# LITTLE CREW OF BUTCHERS

# LITTLE CREW OF BUTCHERS

A NOVEL

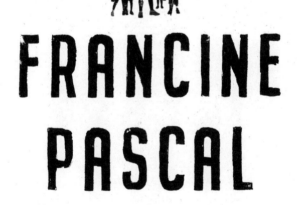

# FRANCINE PASCAL

**BLACK STONE**
PUBLISHING

Published in 2020 by Blackstone Publishing
Cover and book design by Alenka Vdovič Linaschke

Printed in the United States of America

First edition: 2020
ISBN 978-1-982614-76-8
Fiction / General

1 3 5 7 9 10 8 6 4 2

CIP data for this book is available
from the Library of Congress

Blackstone Publishing
31 Mistletoe Rd.
Ashland, OR 97520

www.BlackstonePublishing.com

*To my daughters, Jamie Stewart,*
*Laurie Wenk-Pascal, and Susan Pascal Johansson.*

"A free license given to all acts of inhumanity and lust…this execrable crew of butchers."

*Gulliver's Travels*,
Jonathan Swift

# CHAPTER ONE

Friday, July 1

From Charley Adler's bedroom window, he can see Big Larry with his pilot fish, the vomitous Duncan twins, charging down the street heading right for his house. Instantly, Charley drops down so that he can't be seen from the street. He carefully squiggles up, his nose inching just high enough past the windowsill so he can peek out and see the loathsome threesome pass the house next door. At the rate they're moving, Charley figures they'll be at his house in less than a minute.

Even from this far away, just from his body language, Charley can see that Big Larry is in a mood. And it's not a good one. It's never a good one unless someone's crying. And he's made them do it.

Big Larry is only big to his gang mostly because, at twelve, he's two years older than they are, and he's tall for his age and weighs probably twice as much as they do, a future fat man. He already has a fat man's pink flush to his cheeks and the slit eyes that would one day be crowded even thinner by more fat. That's what makes him Big Larry. It's not like it's all muscle, because it isn't, it's mostly blubber, but it still hurts when he whacks you because there is so much of it.

There's no way Big Larry can know Charley is home if he stays down out of sight. He's not even going to risk peeking again. Last thing Charley wants is to be the one to put the big guy in a good mood 'cause that means he'll be the one doing the crying.

All he has to do is stay where he is and not answer the door. His parents always keep the door locked when they're not home so Larry can't get in. He'll probably ring a few times then figure nobody's home and go away.

And right on cue, the doorbell rings, and then Larry bangs like four times in a row. *Bang, bang, bang, bang.* Hard. Even though it's only a bell, it makes Charley jump because he knows Big Larry is on the other end and he's angry.

What if Big Larry doesn't go away? Suppose he waits for him outside? Then Charley'll have to lie on the floor in his bedroom all day until his parents come home and that's not till five. Still, anything is better than messing with Big Larry and that's even before he knows what he wants.

Charley figures he's safe upstairs and is practically smiling at outfoxing Big Larry even though he's the only one who will ever know that he did.

Just when he's licking his chops, really enjoying his triumph, he remembers.

*Lucy!*

Too late! His stupid little sister is downstairs and she's going to answer the door. But wait. She hates Big Larry even more than Charley does, so maybe she won't let him in.

Or maybe she will. Even though she's three years younger than he is, only seven, you never know what Lucy is going to do. Not ever.

Why does he have to have such a weird sister?

It's quiet downstairs. Maybe she's not opening the door.

"Hey! Charley! Get your ass down here!"

She opened the door.

The game is over for Charley. Nothing to do but get down those stairs quick as he can so's not to make it worse like he was hiding from him—which of course, he was.

Charley takes the stairs two at a time, jumping the last four and pulling at his shorts like he was just coming out of the bathroom.

"Just taking a dump."

"Move it! We're hitting Smilers right now. I need supplies."

"Yeah, c'mon, what's takin' so long?" Suck-up Benny Duncan, the twin with the white hair and stuck-out ears, gets right into it like he's Big Larry's lieutenant or something.

"Yeah, c'mon …" Dennis, the other twin, does an echo thing. He's the taller twin and he has dark hair and one of his eyes is blue and the other one is brown. Some twins; they didn't even look like brothers.

But they do everything Larry says and always agree with him even when they don't mean it. Even so, he's still mean to them. And when he's mean to just one of them, like Benny when he bent his thumb way back, Dennis didn't do anything to stop him.

"Shut up!" Charley can say that to Benny, but he would never dare say it to Big Larry.

"Get a shirt with long sleeves, like a sweatshirt," Larry says.

"But it's hot."

"I told you, we're going to Smilers for supplies. Don't you get it?"

But Charley is so nervous he doesn't get it. Big Larry always makes him so he can't think straight. And in that moment he's starting to panic, and then Lucy pulls at his shirt and whispers, "The sleeves. To put the stuff in."

And then he remembers. "Yeah, I get it," Charley says. "I just didn't know if you wanted sweatshirts for everyone," he makes a stab at a cover-up.

But Big Larry's not buying. "Yeah, right." And to show him how much he's not buying it, he gives him a whack upside the head with the heel of his hand. Hard enough to send Charley falling back into Dennis who slams up against the wall.

"Hey! Watch out!" Dennis shouts and shoves Charley who shoves him back.

"Cool it, you two!" Big Larry says, and then to Charley, "You don't have a sweatshirt, forget it, you're not coming."

Nothing would make Charley happier than not going with Big Larry on the shoplifting caper. He hates doing it, not because it's stealing but because he gets so panicky his hands shake and he's always dropping stuff. He knows he's going to get caught and his parents will go through the roof. Besides, he never steals anything he really wants. Mostly it's little things like screws or washers, whatever they are, or even worse, girl things. He only steals stuff that he can easily scoop up his sleeve. If they get anything good, Big Larry keeps it.

One time, Dennis snatched an electric foot smoother. It was winter and he had on this big down jacket so he shoved it underneath. Even Big Larry made a big deal of it, patting him on the back, probably too hard, but Dennis was over the moon to be the hero of the day. Except nobody could figure out what to do with it so they junked it in the garbage. But first, Big Larry made them destroy it, rip it apart and smash the pieces.

Charley tries to look disappointed about not going with them. And like a good sport, he shrugs, "It's okay, I'll go next time."

And he'd have been in the clear except Lucy, his weirdo sister, is shoving a New York Yankees sweatshirt into his hand.

"Put it on," Big Larry says, "and let's get a move on." And pointing to Lucy, "But not her."

"I gotta bring her," Charley says. "But I'm gonna tell my parents they gotta get a babysitter."

"Yeah, like you didn't say that last week."

Charley would never disagree with Big Larry, but he's answering to a higher power this time. His parents. They both work and during school vacation time, he's Lucy's babysitter.

"You better talk to them tonight. Okay, guys, let's go."

And with Big Larry in the lead, the little band of thieves sets off down the street to walk the five blocks to Smilers Cool Shoppe in the middle of town. After Charley's block, it changes; there's still sidewalk, but on both sides of the street, instead of houses, there are trees.

"Okay, everyone, off the sidewalk and get onto the dirt as close to the trees as you can in case someone is following us, like with a camera," Big Larry says. "They won't be looking for us in the trees."

Nobody asks why anyone would be following them. Everyone, except Lucy, does what he says and gets over into the trees.

"You too." Big Larry points at Lucy.

She keeps walking on the sidewalk where she is and doesn't answer.

So Charley answers for her. "She's not allowed to get off the sidewalk. That's so's she won't walk in the street with the cars."

Big Larry doesn't bother to point out that the trees aren't even near the cars because when it comes to Charley's weirdo sister it's like none of the regular things fit. Most of the time he doesn't even ask her to do anything because she probably won't and it looks bad for him with the other kids.

He hates her. A lot of the time he thinks about pushing her into the cars or off some ledge. He wishes she would get run down by a car.

Like now, he just pretends she's not with them.

With the exception of Lucy, the other four walk as close to the trees and out of sight as possible until they get to the main street in Shorelane, called, appropriately, Main Street, with their target, Smilers Cool Shoppe.

Despite the hip name and the attempt at Bloomingdale's-like counters, it looks a lot like an old five-and-dime from the 1950s. The front window, framed in white-painted wood, is probably the original entrance. After all these years, it has picked up a charm from just being old.

Big Larry stops his gang on the corner.

"Dennis, you take the back of the store with the toothpaste and stuff. Charley, you take the front on the other side."

"That's all girl's stuff."

"So?"

Charley isn't about to argue. He's been borderline, what with his not answering the door and not having the right shirt. And the Lucy thing. He's not going to argue about this. It could be worse. Big Larry could make him go with him, and then he would have to swipe whatever he points to. "Sure," he says. "I got it."

So Benny gets to go with Big Larry.

Bad news. Looking in through the plate glass window, the store is almost empty. It's a lot easier when there are crowds you can hide behind.

"You wait out here and watch for cops," Big Larry tells Lucy like it was a job.

"Uh-uh," she says, shaking her head no.

Even though, like now, Lucy can say no to Larry, she's afraid of him. From where she stands, he's really big, and he always pushes everyone around and everyone is afraid of him. Definitely her brother, and absolutely the Duncan twins. Lucy is scared too, but she doesn't show it the regular way. Still, when Larry is mean to somebody, nobody does anything to stop him. Even though Lucy doesn't like it, she doesn't either.

But sometimes if she really doesn't want to do something Larry says everybody has to do, like now, she would just shake her head no and say, *uh-uh*. Nobody ever tried to talk Lucy into doing something she didn't want to do. Larry would say she was only a girl and too little and so what anyway, and Lucy would just stand there, cross her arms, and stare at him until he moved away.

But that didn't change the fact that inside her stomach was twitching. Like everyone, Larry made her nervous. That's why she always watches him. She watched him so hard that lots of times she would dream about him, dream he was chasing her up a ladder and looking under her skirt and trying to grab her place.

She would like it a lot if Larry got dead, not from something she did, not from anything special—just that one morning he woke up dead. That would be good because maybe then Charley could be the leader of their group and nobody would have to be afraid.

The only reason Lucy hung around with them at all was because of Charley. He was supposed to be taking care of her. Lucy snorted. Like she needed someone to take care of her. Charley needed someone more than she did. And he was more scared of Larry than she was, but the most scared ones were the Duncan twins. Some twins; they didn't look anything alike. She and Charley looked more alike. At least they had the same color red hair.

Larry pushed Charley around a lot too, made him do things he didn't want to do. Sometimes when Larry made him wrestle or they were just fooling around punching each other, Lucy could see Charley's face getting redder and redder. She knew he was going to cry because Larry was so much bigger and stronger, and sometimes he did 'cause it really hurt. And then Larry would do the uncle thing with him, holding him down and making him say uncle before he let him up.

Still, it wasn't anything like what he did with the Duncan twins. They were like his slaves, his toys. They did everything Larry wanted. He would tell them to make a fart or a burp and then crack their knuckles at the same time, and they would. Then he would tell them to do it together and he would lead them like a conductor for an orchestra and they would go crazy trying to keep up.

Actually, that was pretty funny. But it wasn't funny if they didn't do it like he wanted.

One time he stuck a fork in Dennis's arm and it bled and Dennis had to tell his mother and get a tetanus shot. But he never told her how it happened. Alls he said was that he was trying to stick his fork into a grape and he missed.

Another time she heard Dennis talking about how Larry made them all do a circle jerk, a thing where they stood around in a circle and pulled their dick-boys until they peed or something, except Larry was the only one who peed or whatever.

But they only did that when Lucy wasn't there because Charley wouldn't let her see. One time Dennis said Benny's dick-boy got so red from pulling that it started to bleed and he got so scared he ran home crying. Nobody knows what he told their mother that time.

When Lucy would say no to Big Larry, that would scare Charley. Like now.

"Aw, Luce, come on." Charley is almost pleading. "Please wait out here. If you wait inside, you're gonna get me caught."

Lucy's not big on favors, but if she was going to do one for someone, it would probably be Charley, so she says, "Okay."

The four boys, as inconspicuously as possible, go into the variety store one at a time so they don't look like they're together. This, despite the fact that they are all dressed in shorts with long-sleeved sweatshirts and it's almost ninety degrees.

Lucy waits outside, on the alert for cops.

# CHAPTER TWO

Earlier that day, seventy miles west of Shorelane, at the toll booths that line the entrance to the George Washington Bridge, Lucas Baird was on the last leg of his journey hitchhiking from Los Angeles to New York City. Actually, it was more like escaping.

Hitchhiking across the country had been difficult. He was always worried that the cops would pick him up. Once that happened, he was done for. He was a wanted man.

Still, it helped that he was young, twenty-two, and handsome, a face that had lifted all its best features right out of the George Clooney/Brad Pitt gene pool. And he sounded good. His voice was deep and smooth, a light Australian accent with the hard edges polished down by American television, leaving the slightest hint of British.

He was very careful not to look scroungy. He kept his hair short and always tried to have on a clean T-shirt. Still, for the most part, ordinary people were afraid to stop for him, for anyone. Even truck drivers had become more cautious.

It was hot and the noonday sun, with its rich yellow rays, beat down mercilessly through the cloudless early July sky. There had been nowhere on the exposed shoulder of the turnpike for him to hide from its searing heat. With his hand held up to shade his eyes, Luke plodded on, the bridge shimmering like a mirage in the distance. He'd walked the last couple of miles not even bothering to hold up his thumb. It was too hot to go through another bullshit story. Every ride got a new story.

Hell, he'd rather walk.

Once he got to the tollbooths, he figured it would be easy to pick up a lift into the city.

Hitchhiking was illegal at the booths, but the heavy traffic was backed up and slowed to a crawl, providing an advantage for a hitchhiker aiming to work the cars unseen by the attendants or the cops stationed in the area.

When he finally reached the tollbooths, he was right. At least eight people rolled up their windows at his approach. Funny to be thought of as threatening. It was hot and Luke was getting aggravated at the lack of welcome he was getting when he noticed that the collector's booth at the far end was closed and barricaded.

Too tempting to resist.

Under cover of traffic, Luke ducked his way over to the last lane, then nonchalantly lifted the barricade and slipped into the empty booth. With a wave of his hand he directed the traffic over to his lane.

And they came. Happily.

Where did he get this stuff? It had to be in the genes. It was a talent, like playing the piano or tap dancing. Probably passed directly down from good old Dad, a brilliant scam artist who'd scammed his pregnant mother before he took off, never to be seen again.

The first four cars had the sixteen dollars exact, and by the fifth car he was easily changing twenties. It was another three cars before an attendant in the next booth noticed Luke.

"Hey, whatta doin' there?!" he yelled. Leaning out of his booth, he waved over the two policemen standing at the opposite ends of the road. "Hey, Pete, get that guy outta there!"

Pete, the cop, and his partner made their way quickly across the eight lanes to where Luke was swooping up the last sixteen bucks before taking off at top speed toward the bridge.

The two cops cut through the traffic and gave chase. After some minutes of hide-and-seek around the cars, the cops were beginning to close in. They had Luke squeezed in and cornered alongside a Jeep; one blocked the front while the other held the back. But just ahead were open spaces where the traffic was thinning and beginning to move.

Only one way to get there.

Luke took it. Making the break, he scrambled up the back of the Jeep and onto the roof, which by good chance left him exactly at the height of a truck passing on his left. He made the leap, grabbing onto a vertical bar jutting from the back of the truck. His legs swung out as the truck found an opening in the traffic and picked up speed.

Holding tight, Luke pulled in his legs and shimmied up the bar, dropping his feet down and planting himself securely on the narrow ledge at the rear. From there he could reach the metal door handle in the center. With one foot wedged against a steel eye-beam protruding over the bumper, he had enough purchase to lift the door up the few inches he needed to jam his foot underneath.

With one hand on the handle and his foot lifting upward, fighting the speed of the truck all the while, he slid the door open wide enough to allow him to squeeze his body into the darkness of the truck's interior. The police, on foot, were easily outdistanced.

Inside the truck, Luke threw himself back onto what felt like a pile of large, bulging burlap sacks. Thin lines of sunlight breaking here and there through the truck's paneled sides cut the blackness. The air was cold, but felt delightfully cool to Luke's overtaxed, overheated body. He was exhausted, still shaking from the overload of adrenaline shooting through his veins. But he was safe, and it made him smile, the way he'd done it.

He loved the tollbooth scam. He'd always had a creative talent, he just had to find the right channel for it. And New York was going to be the place. And he'd be safe. For now, anyway.

Content to have made it cross-country with just the right amount of excitement, he lay back and made himself as comfortable as he could against the cold, lumpy sacks.

Something sharp struck his back.

An instant later, what felt like a nip just below his shoulder sent Luke leaping to his feet. He spun, searching the darkness for a glimpse of whatever had bitten him. Something was alive in here. Shit!

One of the thin lines of striated sunlight cut lengthwise across the sack he'd been using as a pillow. Even in that little flash, he could see that the sack was moving. Gingerly, Luke leaned in close enough to make out what looked like the point of a greenish-black claw jutting though the torn burlap, viciously snapping its claw jaws open and shut as it worked its way further out through the hole. Swooping down, Luke grabbed the sack by its closed ruffled top and swung it as far away from himself as he could. It hit the far wall of the truck.

The power of the slam split the sides of the sack, sending what looked like a million angry crabs exploding into wild freedom. They scurried with mad speed, sending the panicked Luke scampering to the top of another pile of sacks. But crabs can climb. Luke couldn't see them, but he could hear their hard bodies scratching the floor of the truck as they advanced on him from all directions.

He had to see his enemy. He jumped down from the crest of the sacks and leaped to the sliding door, scrambling for the handles. The crabs nipped at his fingers, but he found the metal bar and, with a great heave, hauled it up far enough to let in the light.

The place was alive with frantic crabs racing and turning every which way, sinking their claws into anything they could find. At least three were hanging onto the bottom of his jeans. He tried to shake them off but they stayed attached. The sons of bitches were nipping at his ankles! Luke ripped them off with his hands and flung them out of the truck onto the highway.

There were too many. He jumped back and, using another sack as a broom, he swept the loose crabs from the truck. Then he tossed the sack.

In the light he could see frenzied movement in the other sacks. No way was he sitting in here with these menacing monsters threatening to break loose. Swinging freely, he emptied the truck of the other sacks.

Behind him on the road, he could hear the awful sound of crunching crustaceans and the screech of tires as cars braked and swerved, trying to avoid the scuttling crabs and lobsters that covered the roadway in all directions.

Luke's last look out of the back of the truck was the sight of a Mercedes neatly slicing off the front bumper of another Mercedes as it veered to avoid the splattered carnage on the road. He slammed down the door.

In the darkness, he trampled every inch of the floor to make certain the truck was completely empty. Satisfied, he pulled his backpack over and, using it as a pillow, lay back, but the lumps in his back pockets kept him from being comfortable so he pulled out his wallet, some useless keys, a pen and a nail clipper and some other pocket crap and shoved it all into his backpack. Exhausted from panic, the monotonous rolling and bumping of the truck quickly put him to sleep.

He slept for almost two hours and only woke because the truck had stopped. Parked, he figured. Carefully and quietly, Luke slid the door up far enough to squeeze his head out. On one side of the road he could see part of an overgrown empty lot. The other side was wooded, but visible up a long driveway was a sprawling one-story clapboard restaurant with a Seafood and Cocktails sign. It wasn't hard to figure out that this had to be the delivery point. The problem was that when the driver came around and saw that his truck was empty, he would probably go berserk. Luke slid out of the truck and ducked behind a small clump of bushes.

He watched as the driver, a solid two-hundred pounder, got out of his truck. The man checked a manifest in his hand, jammed the paper into his breast pocket, and walked around to the back of the truck. Luke felt bad for him. He was going to be mighty upset when he saw the empty truck.

For a moment, Luke's conscience twinged. He hadn't meant to get the driver in trouble, but shit, he couldn't have those little creatures eating him alive, could he?

Just as he'd expected, the guy went nuts when he opened the door.

He couldn't believe his eyes. He jumped up to make sure he wasn't seeing things, or not seeing things. But he was right; there wasn't a lobster or crab in sight. Thirty sacks gone. Disappeared. How could that be? He hadn't stopped long enough for anyone to steal the load—hell, he hadn't even stopped for coffee! Maybe he forgot to pack them. But no, he distinctly remembered struggling to find a way to load it one level so none of the crabs and lobsters would get crushed. What the devil happened? And what was this?

That's when Luke remembered, he hadn't taken his backpack.

The driver picked up the backpack and tore open the zipper. When he saw it was nothing but clothes, he flung it back inside the truck.

Furious, the driver slammed down the door and, like the proverbial barn door, locked it. Too late. Then he stood, hands on his hips, looking around like he expected to see someone come out of the bushes holding his sacks. Nothing. After a couple of minutes, still steaming mad, he walked back to the driver's side and got in.

All of Luke's earthly possessions—and they weren't many—were in the back of that truck.

His only option was to somehow beat the truck to the traffic light ahead and hitch a ride. At least he could find out where the guy was going, then maybe he could find a way to get his stuff back.

Luke, body sunk low in a crouch, ran along the wooded area toward the traffic light. It was a good four-block run, and he was gasping and in a sweat when he got there. Luckily, the truck still hadn't moved. It looked like the driver was just sitting there, probably trying to figure out his next move.

Luke got to the light and looked back.

With his thumb out and the most benign look he could muster on his face, Luke waited. Finally, he saw the truck begin to move. Slowly. Probably he'd spotted Luke and was going to stop for him.

About a block away the guy put on his left signal and Luke realized he was going to make the left turn before the light. That's when he started running. But he didn't make it. The truck took the turn and was two hundred feet down the road by the time Luke got to the corner.

Every goddamn thing he had left in the world was on that truck. Everything. All his bullshit résumés, his one credit card, his driver's license, his expired passport, telephone numbers, cell phone, everything. Plus almost five hundred dollars, not counting the sixty-four bucks from the tollbooth. Luke dug into his pockets and came up with a fiver and some change. He was as good as broke. On his ass. Down and out in wherever the hell he was.

Shorelane.

That's what the road sign said. Where the hell was Shorelane? He started walking. A few hundred feet ahead he saw another sign that pointed to I-495, under which it said "Long Island Expressway." Luke had never been out East before, but he'd heard about Long Island and Fire Island and the Hamptons. They talked about those places in LA. A lot of the important people he'd met, the ones who originally came from the East and considered themselves intellectuals, had summer homes on Long Island.

But, though Luke couldn't have known, not in Shorelane. Shorelane was a small town, about fifteen thousand people in winter and, surprisingly, not many more in the summer. Even though it was on the Great South Bay, it didn't seem to attract summer tourists, perhaps because no one had built up summer accommodations. A tall hotel would have violated zoning laws; motels would have been permissible, but no new ones had been built in the last twenty-five years. The old ones were marginal, ordinary to shabby, used mostly for daytime trysts by people from bigger towns like Hempstead. It was safe to assume that if you were from any chic place on Long Island, you would not run into anyone you knew in Shorelane.

Luke walked along the macadam road, now bordered on both

sides by acres of flat, neatly rowed farmland. After about a mile, the landscape changed to low-story office buildings interspersed with drive-in fast-food huts, gas stations, used-car lots, and topless bars. He used seventy-five cents to buy a soda at a Shell station.

It was midafternoon now and the streets were almost empty. The working people were back in their offices and shops, teens were at the beaches, and mothers with babies were catching a quick after-lunch rest before their older children came home and dinner preparations began. Only wanderers, people with no purpose, people like Luke, were on the street, and there were very few of them.

The street took a slant uphill and became Main Street. As he came closer to the top of the hill, he could look down on the center of the town of Shorelane, a dinky, ordinary town.

As he came closer, he could see what looked an old five-and-dime from the 1950s. He saw a store exactly like it in LA last year, on a movie set for a TV film set just before the Second World War. He was a "townspeople" extra, so he had plenty of time to wander around.

The shop today in Shorelane was real and almost identical to the movie set, except it was neat and shabby where the other had been new and shiny. He'd actually been on his way up the street to the bar, but he felt he could use a little sprucing up. For that he needed his comb and toothbrush which, of course, were in his lost knapsack. So he turned into Smilers Cool Shoppe, past a little red-headed girl crouched, as only small children can do, without her bottom touching the sidewalk and her arms wrapped around her knees.

# CHAPTER THREE

Before Luke has been in the store for two minutes, he has pocketed the perfect comb. Heading for toothbrushes, he passes another counter with hair dyes.

Sometimes people asked him about the blond streaks in his hair. From the time he was sixteen and his blond hair had begun to darken, he'd always had lighter streaks. When he was out in LA with that powerful sun, they turned yellow. With his tan, they looked great. Even Luke liked them. But now, here in New York, without the California sun … Luke studies the possibilities and finds they have boxes just for streaks.

"May I help you?"

The counter girl is the kind you would see in a movie, except this time, she's real. Tall and slim with perfect out-of-focus Breck-girl blond curls that just touch her shoulders. If she's wearing makeup, it's ideal, invisible in itself but magically blushing her cheeks, long brown lashes that encircle oval-shaped eyes, light-brown pupils flecked with yellow, making the fusion hazel to olive.

Gentle eyes that you could relax into, and the rest of her face is just as sweet. Her voice suits her with its soft, almost whispery sound.

Perfect as she appears on close examination, when you pull back, nothing about her face is sharp or strong enough to claim real beauty. Delicate is the definitive word.

"What do you think?" Luke asks. "What I mean is, can you match me up? The streaks, I mean."

"Oh, I see. Well, what did you use before?"

"Nothing. These are real, but I was in LA. Not going to get that kind of sun in New York, right? What did you say your name was?"

"Daisy Rumkin."

"Lucas Barnes," saying the first name he could think of. At least he stayed with the initials.

"Are you an actor?"

"Yeah, just starting. Did you see *Walking Wonders* with Gwyneth Paltrow?"

Of course, Daisy couldn't possibly have seen the nonexistent movie he just made up on the spot, but she's captivated nonetheless. Here she is in Shorelane, Long Island, the dead-end place she hates most in the world, and a movie star comes in and talks to her. Daisy steals a quick glance around, hoping some of the other girls are watching. But no one is.

"I love Gwyneth Paltrow and I would see anything she's in. Is it playing here?"

There he goes again. Luke watches himself easing into the lie. Hey, what was he going to do? Tell her who he really is? An Australian nobody, drifting in from LA? Or worse, running from the LA cops. That would be a winner. He is attracted to this girl, really likes her right away. It's that kind of electric connection that rarely happens. If it's big enough, they call it "love at first sight."

So, Luke uses the only talent he has—his quick mouth—and by the time he's finished, he has a date with her for a picnic on the beach tonight.

"I get off at five." She says, "You can pick me up here."

"Later," he says. Waving, he walks off, going back to his not-exactly-shopping.

Meanwhile, at the back of the store, the twin, Benny, from the gang of little kids, is busy pretending to be studying the dental supplies and doesn't even notice Big Larry come up behind him.

"Nobody's around, and you still got nothin'?" Big Larry says shoving him out of the way. "Watch this."

Pulling his sweatshirt sleeve down practically over his hand, Larry reaches for the last tube of Crest toothpaste. Just at the same moment, a larger hand shoves his out of the way.

"Uh-uh, sonny," Luke says, shoving Larry's hand away and palming the toothpaste and sliding it off the counter and into his pocket. To make amends, he puts a friendly hand on Larry's shoulder, winks, and smiles down at him.

"Hey, mister, get ya hand offa me!" Larry whips himself out from under Luke's hand, not one bit intimidated by the repri-mand of an adult. Especially one who has to shoplift himself.

"It's okay, kid, just a joke," Luke whispers under his breath, then winks like Larry is in on the joke.

The guy is big, and Larry isn't about to take any chances, so he shrugs his shoulders in an effort to keep some of his tough-guy dignity in front of his gang and walks away.

Luke watches him make his way over to a knot of kids, all of them smaller than him. He can see him telling his friends what happened, even pointing in his direction. The other kids look over at Luke. Even from across the store he can see their faces screwed up into hostile squints.

Screw 'em, Luke thinks as he heads toward the exit in the front of the store. Just as he's passing the last counter before the exit, he hears a ruckus behind him and when he turns, he sees that a man in a white shirt, obviously a manager-type, has the big kid and one of the other boys by the shoulders of their sweatshirts. Luke is close enough to see that the man is very angry, and the kids are scared.

"It's that guy over there! He said we should! He did it too!" Larry is shouting.

By now, Lucy, the little redhead from outside, has come into the store. Sensing trouble, she walks over to her brother, Charley.

"Stop that man!" the manager calls out, and another man, a shopper, and one of the other saleswomen steps in front of Luke, effectively blocking his way to the street.

"Hey, what's happening?"

"You," the manager says, pointing to Luke, "step over here, please."

"Sure, no problem." Luke immediately starts walking over to the group of kids. As he does, he makes way for a saleswoman to pass in front of him, in the process accidentally bumping into the candy counter and knocking off a few chocolate bars. "Excuse me," he says to the saleswoman, picking up the fallen items and replacing them on the counter.

"That guy," Larry points at Luke, "he made us do it. Said he was gonna give us half price for anything we lifted."

Everyone turns to Luke, the stranger, who turns to his accuser. "It's okay, kid, I said I wouldn't tell on you, didn't I?" His voice is calming and gentle. "But I did say you shouldn't do that anymore." Now he turns into the stern father. "I told you you were going to get in trouble, and see, you did."

By now Larry's face has become bright red, caught between fury and tears. He shouts, "He's a liar! I seen 'im steal some toothpaste. He shoved it in his pocket. Ya could look. Go on, look in his pockets!"

Luke turns to the adults and shrugs, giving them an embarrassed smile, embarrassed more for the boy than for himself. He lifts his arms as if to say, go ahead, take a look. Be my guest.

The manager is uncomfortable, but he has to quiet the boy who is now close to hysterics and shouting at the top of his lungs. "He took it! Look in his pockets!"

"Yeah, I saw 'im too," Dennis joins in.

The manager excuses himself to Luke and gingerly pats at his jacket pockets and then the pockets in his pants. At which point, Luke stops him and, putting his hands in his pants pockets, takes out the few dollars he has along with some coins and then proceeds to pull the linings inside out. Of course, his pockets are empty. The pilfered merchandise was dumped when he "accidentally" bumped into the chocolate counter.

Now Larry is crying in earnest. Blubbering about how he'd seen Luke do it.

But Luke, Mr. Nice Guy, smiles down at the boy, not the smirk of a victor, but the kind smile of an understanding adult. Actually, he does feel a little sorry for the kid, but he can't afford any trouble.

"Come on, Mac," Luke appeals to the manager on Larry's behalf. "He didn't mean any harm. They're just kids. You know, out for a little excitement. Right, kids? Tell him you're not going to do it again, okay?"

Now there are five children, counting Larry and the little girl from outside the store. The children are frightened and confused and grab the first way out. "No." They shake their heads. "Never ..."

But Larry is having trouble. He's still sobbing.

"Come on, son." Luke turns to the crying boy. "It's okay. I'm not angry." And then to the manager and the other sales help who have abandoned their counters to gather around the action. By now even Daisy is there watching and he's playing to her. "He didn't mean to lie. He was just scared. How about giving them all one more chance?"

"Well ..." The manager pretends to be thinking it over. "This man's been such a good sport, I think if he gets an apology from you that'll be enough for me. Providing I don't see you around for a while. Okay, kids?"

All except for Larry shake their heads in agreement. But Larry isn't buying it.

"Let's hear it, young man," the manager says, but Larry won't budge. "Unless you want me to call your dad."

That does it. Fear overtakes outrage, and Larry mumbles a sorry someplace in Luke's direction.

Luke munificently accepts the apology and has smiles in all directions as he heads out the door. He's pushed his luck far enough. He can hear the manager launching into a sermon on honesty and truthfulness that promises to go on for a good while.

# CHAPTER FOUR

Luke sees Daisy coming up the street. The late-afternoon sun is behind her, low light outlining her slim body under her thin cotton dress and shining through her hair, whitening the blond blur of ringlets. Her dress isn't LA short; rather, it falls just a little above the knee. Her shoulder-length hair is pinned in a style that could have easily worked just as well eighty years earlier. Except for the plastic bag she's carrying, Daisy would fit perfectly into that 1940s movie he worked on.

He likes her look. More than he expected. For a moment he regrets his bullshit.

When Daisy sees Luke, she smiles. He walks toward her, surprised at how excited he really is. He reaches for the plastic bag she's holding and finds it heavier than he expected.

"This feels like dinner for four," he jokes, holding it up to measure the weight.

"It's the water. I probably got too much. A gallon jug. That was dumb, huh?" The sweetness of her tone adds to her fragility.

"Hey, no, I'm a big water drinker. And it's great with Stoli, too." The alcohol, compliments of the liquor store guy who was too busy with a customer to notice the guy browsing through the vodkas. Luke wasn't happy to have done it, but it couldn't be helped. "You like vodka?"

She nods her head with the polite enthusiasm of a nondrinker. Too bad, Luke thinks, liquor makes everything easier. And, looking at her, her light dress whispering against her skin, he really wants it to be easy. More than that, he wants to make love to her.

"C'mon," he says, taking her arm. "Show me the beach. I'm getting thirsty."

Together they cross Main Street and walk down an alley to the woods behind the stores. Luke does most of the talking, nice, gentle talking, the kind that seems to ask questions that don't need answers. But he does learn that Daisy's parents divorced when she was seven, that she has a younger brother who lives with her father in San Diego, a father she hadn't seen in over five years and a brother she hadn't seen for almost fifteen. Her mother had died five years earlier, which was the reason for her father's visit. He came to the funeral mainly because he thought maybe he might be a beneficiary of some insurance policy he'd taken out years before. Turned out her mother had cashed it in as soon as he walked out.

There's a strange lack of bitterness or anger in Daisy's voice; she gives a simple, nonjudgmental recounting of a sad, quiet life without many choices.

Rather than spoil the mood with bullshit stories, Luke talks about his hometown in Australia. Nostalgic memories of kind moments. Not the wildness of teenage life, just the turning leaves and the good smell of autumn air, the colors and the peace.

Their memories are similar. It makes them feel close.

They walk for about ten minutes until they reach a sandy beach bordering the bay. Next to the sign with all the prohibitions—no pets, no skating, no littering, no bikes—is a sign warning visitors that the beach would be closed until July 15 for reconstruction. A half-hearted line of green plastic fence extends for about one hundred feet along the shoreline.

Daisy smiles. "It's okay; they're not working at night."

"What are they doing?"

"See all that metal stuff? They're building a sea wall and a jetty to save the town's main beach."

Like all inland-waterway beaches, this one is rocky with clumps of weeds and a mixture of dirt and sand. With the exception of two fishermen on a distant pier, they are alone. Luke leads Daisy past the construction to a sheltered nook where the beach curves into a small, weedy dune.

"I didn't have time to go home," Daisy apologizes, "so I couldn't get a blanket. I hope it's all right …"

"Okay for me. Here, you take this." Luke slips out of his windbreaker and spreads it on the sand for her.

Daisy settles on the smallest corner of the jacket. Luke chooses a piece of sand just alongside and adjusts the rest of the jacket underneath her.

"How about cups? Did you bring any?"

Daisy reaches for the Dixie cups in her plastic bag and takes out the gallon bottle of Poland Spring water, paper napkins, and her prize contribution, a tube of Pringles. "For hors d'oeuvres," she says.

"Great." Luke pours her a good-sized cup of vodka. "Don't worry; it's only a Dixie cup. À votre santé," Luke says, lifting his full cup. Daisy mirrors him.

"Yes, sant*ay*."

They drink, Luke taking a healthy swallow while Daisy barely wets her lips.

"I guess I'm just not a drinker. I'm sorry."

"Don't worry about it. I'll make up for it."

"I brought sandwiches. You like baloney?"

"Love baloney. Could live on it."

"You're teasing me. I know it was dumb bringing something like baloney with you being a movie star and all, but the ham looked so gray …"

"Hey, forget about that stuff. I'm a regular guy—like you, only not so beautiful."

Daisy blushes and mumbles something about Luke being very handsome.

He can see Daisy is nervous. The kind of nervous where you can't stop talking. She's going on how her friends at Smilers had kidded her about going out with a movie star and did he mind that she had told them he was a movie star? Before he can answer, she dives on, her mellifluous voice sprinkling the air with words that dance lightly over the gentle splash of the bay. After a while Luke lets his mind wander to where his eyes are playing, past the few sailboats and out to the empty horizon.

Just seven days ago he was in Malibu, on the beach, watching the heavy monotony of powerful waves breaking and sending the waiting surfers sliding over the top. From the distance, the surfers were like sticks being knocked about, going under, popping up again. Like LA itself, no feel of people at all.

But here, on this ordinary little beach, even the distant fishermen seem personal. The people in the boats, too small to actually make out, probably belong to Shorelane; certainly the fishermen do.

And Daisy does, too.

"You like it here?" he asks.

"Not so much, but I've lived all my life in Shorelane. Never went to college, babysat with the same family for five years, and now I work at Smilers. I suppose the only way to change that is to get out of here."

Daisy turns and finds Luke's face closer to hers than she expects. She pulls back and smiles, not the polite smile and not the humorous smile, but a smile with intimacy and a promise. But she doesn't say anything. Instead, she looks down and begins to unpack the picnic.

"So why don't you?" he asks.

"And go where? I told you, I'm not prepared for anything. You can't just pick up and go when you've got nothing to offer."

She's caught him. Nailed him perfectly without even knowing it. "Hey, you're smart, you're beautiful. Give yourself a chance. Don't say no before you even try." And then he goes too far; he doesn't mean to, but he wants to stay in touch with this girl, and the words slip out before he can think.

"Maybe I can help you."

"Oh my god. You would do that?"

"Sure. Why not? I think you're terrific."

Maybe he can help her. It wouldn't be as a movie star but as someone who has plenty of experience and isn't stupid. And someone who cares. It doesn't seem like there's anyone in her life who cares. Goddamn it, why *shouldn't* he help her?

Daisy is overcome with gratitude. She can barely raise her eyes to look at Luke. To cover her embarrassment, she busies herself with the picnic.

Luke reaches out and touches her hair lightly. She doesn't

seem to notice, just hands him a sandwich. He can see through the plastic that it is, as promised, baloney.

He's surprised at how much he likes Daisy. *Daisy.* He even likes the name.

"Do you like being an actor?" she asks.

"Actually, no. In fact, I don't know if I'm going back to LA."

She's shocked. "You're going to walk away from Hollywood?"

"Before it walks away from me. I don't have a real talent for it. Not like some of those guys; they live and breathe and eat it. To tell you the truth, it always embarrasses me a little."

It's a truth he hasn't told himself before, but something about Daisy makes him want to be open. She's so straight that to lie would be like shooting fish in a barrel. He knows he could say anything, but somehow he doesn't want to.

"What *do* you want to do?"

"Right now?" It's more a caress than a question. He puts his hands on her shoulders lightly, feeling her warm skin under the soft, thin cotton of her dress. He lets his hands run down her silky arms, come to rest on top of her hands, which are splayed on either side of her body holding her upright. She says nothing. She has no choice but to look into his face, inches away, his dark-blue eyes trapping hers.

Gently, he pulls her in until he can feel her breasts against his chest and the fullness of her lips spreading on his. In that instant, in the brief second it takes for the charge of heat to speed along the nerve lines to her sexual corners, Daisy clenches her arms around Luke and presses her open lips hard against his, taking his tongue deep inside her mouth.

And then they're scrambling and grabbing and holding each other, hands and mouths and bodies hungry for contact.

Frantically, they tear at their clothes until their bodies, naked and burning, are pressed against each other and find their fit.

Just at the penultimate moment, something hits the side of Luke's head hard enough to stun him, to whip his head sideways. To stop him.

Daisy opens her eyes.

"What happened?"

And then she sees the thin line of blood trickling from the skin just past Luke's eye. "Oh my god!" She sits up, his penis still inside her, and reaches out for him. It's then that the rain of pebbles begins pelting both of them.

Daisy pulls away from Luke and rolls over, wrapping her arms around her head to escape the cascade of stones. Luke hunches his shoulders, burying his chin in his chest, all the while covering Daisy with his body, protecting as much of her as he can.

Then they hear the shouts and high-pitched wild screams of laughter. The pebbles keep pummeling them, nipping at Luke's back and buttocks and bouncing off his head.

"Sons of bitches! Cut that out!" Luke shouts, covering his face with his hands as he struggles to see his attackers.

From under his arms, he sees them, not ten feet away. The five little kids from town, from Daisy's store. The ones he had the shoplifting contretemps with. Just little kids. Luke begins to rise from his crouching position, still holding his hands over his face.

"Stop that, you little bastards, before I rip your friggin' arms off! Get outta here!" He lunges toward them, and as he does they spin and scramble away like crabs, scattering over the beach. Luke stands there, naked, roaring and flailing in all directions like an impotent Goliath monster, but the kids are safely beyond his reach. He makes a running movement toward the big one and they all take off; within moments, they are out of sight.

"Damn bastards!" he curses, kicking at the sand and mumbling as he makes his way back to Daisy. She's up, dressed, and searching for her shoes.

"Those little creeps! Don't worry, they're gone." Luke sits down next to her. "It's okay."

"It's not okay," Daisy says. "I know them. Every one of them, and their folks. God!" She finds her shoes and slips them on. "I have to go! I have to get out of here! I'm sorry …"

And with that, she takes off, racing over the dunes and disappearing, leaving Luke standing, stupidly naked, alone and out-of-his-mind mad.

He shoves his legs into his pants, almost ripping through the seam in his anger, throws on his shirt, and curses as he sits down on the sand harder than he means to.

"Shit!" he says, and takes a long, long drink of the vodka.

# CHAPTER FIVE

Daisy doesn't stop running until she hits the alley behind Main Street. The lightning and thunder accelerate her flight to a mad dash. A hard, heavy two-minute cloudburst catches her crossing the parking lot behind the beach. She's instantly drenched, but she keeps running. Only beneath the safety of the Main Street buildings does she slow down. Staying close to the brick walls, she peeks out to look for any trace of the children. Nothing.

Walking quickly, she heads up Main to Pocker Road and home. The horror of the beach scene plagues her steps; her mind recounts over and over the sight of the children standing, watching her having sex with a near stranger, someone she had only met that afternoon. And there they were, just like the description she had read one time, "the beast with two backs."

What a hideous beast they must have been for those young children. A lasting, scarring memory like the one Daisy had from when she was eleven and her ex-babysitter described her wedding night, the terrible soreness, how she could barely sit on a chair afterward. The story gave Daisy years of worry until at last she had her own experience—and had no trouble sitting down.

Walking faster now that the rain has stopped, a slim hope presents itself: maybe they hadn't recognized her. She was lying down, and when they started throwing the rocks she had rolled over and covered her face. But the opposing argument made more sense. The children were less than ten feet away, almost on top of them, and on higher ground. God knows how long they had been watching. Additionally, it was still light and they had seen her in the store that very afternoon.

What was she thinking? They knew her. There was no anonymity in Shorelane. Shit!

All the delicious passion of the evening turns rancid. It's become a disgusting spectacle, and Daisy thinks that she'll probably be stuck reliving the nightmare reality for weeks, months, perhaps forever.

But oh, how sweet it was. God, she liked him. Even if he wasn't a movie star, she would have liked him. He threw his body over hers to protect her from the stones hurled by the children. Hero stuff in Daisy's book. Too bad the evening was hopelessly ruined right along with her reputation.

Daisy wonders where is Luke staying. He didn't mention a hotel or friends. What difference does it make? By now he's long gone from Shorelane, and she'll never see him again.

As Daisy walks up her street, she sees her landlady, Mrs. Mc-Donnell, sitting on the porch. Probably listening to the radio; certainly crocheting. She couldn't have heard the gossip yet. It's been only fifteen minutes at most since it happened.

But Mrs. McDonnell will know soon enough. Shorelane is just *that* provincial. Despite the fact that it's on Long Island and not that many miles from New York City, it's a world away in desirability, unhappily situated in the flat nowhere of the South Shore. Not close enough to the city to be a suburb, and not near enough to the Hamptons to be chic.

Daisy checks her dress, making certain it's closed in the back. The bottom of her skirt is wrinkled and wet, but it doesn't look much different than it would on a normal hot working day if you got caught in a downpour. All perfect—except that it's inside out.

# CHAPTER SIX

All Lucy wanted her brother to tell her was how come the man kept jumping up and down on Daisy if all they were doing was sexing? At ten, three years older than Lucy, Charley knew everything when it came to sex. He knew all the ways you could do it. Like a man could stick his thing into a lady's place. Lucy knew that her special place for making a baby was really her belly button. Nobody told her, she just knew.

That always bothered Lucy, how a thing like a penis—she always called the dick-boy a penis because that's what her mother said you were supposed to do, but when she talked to Charley he said it was his dick-boy—how could it squeeze into such a little place like a belly button? Maybe the button un-hooked and there was a pocket the dick-boy, the penis, could fit right in. That's what she figured. But that still didn't explain why the man was jumping on Daisy. Maybe the button was stuck. Or there were other things in the pocket.

Another thing: she didn't like that the man got to be on top;

that was scary. He was a lot bigger than Daisy and could squash her. Lucy liked Daisy and didn't want her to get hurt.

And how come they had to take off all their clothes? She wasn't ever going to do that, take off her clothes in front of a man. Okay, with Charley or her daddy, but not with a real man.

But most of all not with Larry. She hated Larry. One time when he was over playing with her brother, Charley had to go to the bathroom. While he was out of the room, Larry tried to make Lucy show him her place. She said no, and he said if she didn't, he'd hurt her. She remembered him standing real close, practically on top of her. Looking up at his disgusting face with a glob of yellow goo in the corner of his eye and his chapped lips with the peeling skin, she'd told him, You just try. And he said, Maybe I will.

But he didn't. He went off pretending like he didn't care.

With all Larry's meanness to Charley and Benny and Dennis, Lucy thought it was good what happened to Larry at the Smilers Cool Shoppe.

Lucy knew that the man was lying; she saw him put the toothpaste back on the counter when he picked up the candy. Still, she liked it when he got Larry in trouble. They all liked it, even though the Duncan twins pretended they were on Larry's side.

That man, the one from Smilers, was the one sexing Daisy. They saw his butt. And when he got up to chase them they saw his dick-boy and it was gigantic and sticking out like a handle. They all ran like crazy.

When they were safely far enough away, Larry stopped them and told them that they were all going back down to the beach tomorrow to look for that guy again. He said he had a plan. He was going to bring a big fishing net and they were gonna capture him. Gonna show him that he can't mess with us.

But when they get home, Charley tells Lucy that they aren't going to go to the beach and that Larry is an asshole and full of you-know-what and that they're just kids and we can't capture a full-grown man. And he says we're not going to try either.

"Just let him make me," he says.

\* \* \*

That's right after they get home. Charley can hardly speak he's so out of breath from running. So is Lucy, but Charley is scared, too, and Lucy isn't so much. Charley doesn't eat much dinner and their mother wants to know if he's sick, but he says he isn't, so she just feels his head and doesn't take his temperature.

# CHAPTER SEVEN

Three hours later, it's almost bedtime and Lucy is already in her pajamas. All she has to do is brush her teeth, but if no one remembers to make her, she could go to bed without doing it.

The hall phone begins to ring. Lucy doesn't want to stop what she's doing. She's working on a large piece of construction paper painting a horse she had drawn earlier. Her watercolors are lined up beside her and she's just starting to mix the brown. Her easel with its open paint jars, a birthday present from Mom and Dad, is wedged between her and the door. Charley will have to answer it.

Lucy is very good at art. It's her favorite subject and she knows she's going to be an artist when she grows up. Everyone says so. Even at seven, her paintings and drawings are so good they hang all over the house. Some of them even have real frames. She's especially good at holding pictures in her head, and tonight she's painting the horse from memory. She had seen it the week before from the car when they were on their way to Montauk Point. It was behind a white picket fence in a meadow alongside the road. The weekend traffic was tied up for about fifteen minutes, giving her a good chance to study the horse. She could tell it was a mother because of the little baby horse that kept trying to lean against its legs. Just like Lucy did with her mother sometimes when she was embarrassed or shy.

But Lucy doesn't like the way she drew the horse. Its hooves don't sit right on the ground. She plans to hang it on the back of the door so no one will see it.

Her bedroom is right near the hall table and the upstairs phone. She can hear Charley and right away she knows he's talking to Larry. It's the way he keeps saying yes to everything. Not the word yes, but things like uh-huh, sure, right, great idea. She can just see Charley nodding his head up and down even when he isn't speaking. Then he says, "Okay, yeah, tomorrow, I know. Around ten on the beach."

Larry must have asked him something else because he says he doesn't have any rope except Lucy's jump rope. Larry must have said bring it because then Charley says, "Okay, I'll bring it."

Lucy runs to her closet and stands on tiptoes on her wooden paint box until she's tall enough to reach up and grab one end of her jump rope. She slides it off the shelf and shoves it under her bed.

Then she goes back to painting her horse.

# CHAPTER EIGHT

It's a lifetime later—or at least six hours. Luke sits on the small spit of gray shale beach, long dry from the quick downpour, rocking back and forth, drunk and angry.

"Goddamn little shits!" he shouts, punctuating the words with fist slams on the sand of the empty beach. He does this three, four, five times.

Then his hand hits some small rocks.

"Ow!"

It hurts. He blows on his hand and shakes it in the air. The bruised side burns with pain. He tries to soothe it against the cool wet sides of the Stolichnaya bottle. When that doesn't help, he settles for the internal succor of a long swallow of vodka. It seems to quiet him. He leans forward, resting his head on his knees.

The night is still. A warm and humid tent of thick air hangs over him. The only sound is the gentle splash of the bay as it spills lightly, hypnotically, onto the shore. The noise lulls his angst into the woolly softness of a heavy, drunken sleep.

Minutes pass. Without warning, an ear-splitting clap of thunder blasts the stillness. Luke jolts up, arms akimbo, chest leading into the air as if shot by a high-powered rifle. Almost simultaneously, fat pellets of rain begin to fall. They fall hard, making Luke jump unsteadily to his feet.

He is very drunk.

He looks around for shelter; not a hundred feet away the mouth of a large rain sewer looms. Unlike sanitary sewers that carry city waste, these sewers only carry runoff rainwater through openings at least ten or twelve feet high. The pipe looks more like a small cave, with ample diameter to give shelter.

Luke grabs the vodka bottle in one hand and the gallon jug of water in the other. Weaving crazily across the sand, falling to his knees, and pulling himself up again, he makes his way to the gaping opening. Just as he closes in on safety, another clap of thunder sends him sprawling to the ground as an enormous bolt of lightning flashes the night to day. The water jug flies from his hand, but he holds tight to the vodka.

Dazed and out of breath from the outburst of drunken energy, he crawls the last five feet, dragging his body into the sewer.

The few drops of rain stop as abruptly as they started. Yet, the general accumulation from the miles of pipe that feed into the main line and down to the sewer is enough to send a small rivulet of rainwater running through and into a waiting bed in the sand. From there, it flows on into the bay.

Inside the sewer, safe from the elements, all Luke wants is do is go back to sleep.

The breeze outside has cleared the sky; a triangle of moonlight falls into the opening, casting enough light for Luke to find a dry bed on the sandy floor. He takes off his jacket and rolls it into a pillow, but he's so wobbly from the alcohol that it takes him four tries before he can get it positioned under his head. When he finally does, he lies down with thoughts of Daisy, the lovely Daisy, her full heavy breasts generously out of balance with her tiny waist and the silky feel of her skin. Her image sways before him as he passes out.

# CHAPTER NINE

Luke sleeps in the rain sewer without moving as the peaceful night passes into the early morning. From time to time, a nearby train rumbles by, shaking the concrete walls of the sewer and sending a gentle tremor through the ground, but the sound is never sharp enough to disturb Luke or make him change position.

But it's enough to shudder a cluster of wooden beams that are shoring up some temporary cement work above his head. Each time a train passes, the slight back-and-forth movement of the beams pulls them a little farther away from the cement ledge against which they have been wedged.

Around five a.m., a long freight train thunders by at great speed. One of the four-by-eights dislodges fully and swings out over the sleeping man, knocking a second beam out with it. As the far ends of the beams rip from the ceiling, they pull long slabs of concrete out after them.

An instant before the debris strikes, Luke hears the loud cracking sounds. His eyes shoot open just in time to see what looks like the entire ceiling hurtling down onto him with its lethal weight.

He screams when the wood and cement hit him, first from fright and then from agony. From the neck down he feels his body flatten under the terrible weight and he hears his own howl far off in the cavernous sewer, hears it drifting away into an elongated echo. When that sound ends, a new scream starts. The pain tears through his brain. The heavy beams push down, suffocating him, pinning him so that he can't move.

He feels a thick heaviness dragging him down, his body sinking slowly into numbness. The open space below him grows deeper and hazier and then softer and blacker until the pain dulls to pins and needles and Luke collapses down inside himself.

Like a dead man, is his penultimate thought. Then …

*Help me … Please, I don't want to die.*

# CHAPTER TEN

SATURDAY, JULY 2

The first awareness Luke has is the feeling that he is crawling, dragging himself along a deep, dark tunnel. His feet are cemented in lead boots so heavy he has to use his arms to pull the weight of his body, but the walls are too slippery to grab and under him the seaweed is wet and slimy. He keeps sliding backward.

Ahead, deep shades of red begin to streak the sides of the tunnel. He can see pinpoints of colored lights in the distance. He has made no progress, but still the distance comes closer, and the lights brighten and spread in all directions until everything is washed by a glaring whiteness so harsh that his eyes snap open to escape it, thrusting him abruptly into daylight. For an instant there is no feeling at all.

And then the pain punches in.

It shoots to his brain, exploding in his body with each breath. First it comes from his legs, the worst of it concentrated along the back of his calves; when he tries to flex those muscles, there is a sharp pinching at the top of his thighs. When Luke tries to move his arm, a bolt of pain courses up his spine and buries itself like a spear in his shoulder. Inside his brain, pounding against the wall of his skull, is a hammer of white heat. And all over his body there is a weight, a million pounds pinning him against the earth.

But through the pain that tears at his body there is an even greater surge of relief. And it comes in a charge so strong it brings tears to Luke's eyes. He is alive!

But he can't move. With the exception of his left arm below the elbow and his head, his body is pinned under a terrible weight. His feet can turn somewhat from side to side and his right hand, up to the wrist, is free, but every other part of him is locked in.

Luke wiggles his toes. It's painful, but there is movement. And movement in both his hands. He can raise his head high enough off the ground to see around, but his view is blocked by a beam, black with creosote, lying not six inches from his chin. The beam is angled across his chest, reaching down from his right shoulder to where he cannot see. From the feel of the weight, it runs all the way down his legs.

And that isn't the only thing holding him. A slab of cement presses on his left arm just above the elbow. But he can still bend the lower part of his arm.

Rubble and beams must have fallen sometime during the night and are holding him down. But he isn't paralyzed. Luke's sure of that. All his extremities can move. He's seen enough movies and television shows to know that if you have nerve damage, you can't feel your toes and fingers, much less move them.

Maybe he's lucky. Maybe he hasn't even broken anything. After all, he's young and in good shape. From the feel of the weight, it would be a miracle, but he's lying on soft sand, and that might have helped absorb the blow. That same softness gives him a bit of leeway beneath the debris, but moving anything is still too painful. Additionally, Luke can't tell if he's bleeding. That's the real danger: it could take hours for him to be rescued; by that time, he could bleed to death.

The pain begins to recede as Luke's panic grows. The thought of bleeding to death is terrifying. He lifts his head, straining to see where he is, if there's any blood. He can't see any. He tries to ease his head over to the side to look beyond the beam but another pile of cement blocks that view as well.

On either side of him, at least six feet away, he can see the rounded walls of what looks like a gigantic tunnel. The rain sewer. He went in to hide from the storm. After Daisy, the picnic—and those lousy kids.

But what happened after? It's totally wiped out. No memory at all. Luke thinks maybe the beams hit his head, but then he turns to the other side and sees the bottom of the empty vodka bottle.

Ah yes.

It's all coming back. Yes, he definitely remembers Daisy. And at the same time, he remembers those goddamn kids! Just the thought of those little bastards brings a nice, healthy anger that helps quiet the panic he feels about possibly bleeding to death.

With the panic quieted, exhaustion takes over, and Luke falls back to sleep.

# CHAPTER ELEVEN

A sharp pain shoots through Luke's chest, waking him up to reality. With the free part of his left arm, he tries to push away the cement that has pinned the top half of his body, but it's a huge slab that must weigh fifty pounds. He can't get any purchase. When he tries to push the beam that crosses his chest, he has no luck either.

He tries to burrow his other arm into the sand to work it out from under the beam but is stopped by a sharp piece of wood that threatens to cut into his arm.

At least he's facing the right direction, toward the opening to the beach. It's light enough now, probably sixish. He is maybe twenty feet from the entrance, but the opening is big enough so that a passerby could see him if they look in the right direction. At least they can see the pile of wood and cement and maybe his feet.

If they can't see him, he realizes, they can certainly hear him. That's when he starts to shout. The echo helps. For every one shout he gets two back. Sure, it's early, but fishermen start at the crack of dawn, don't they? He'd seen those two fishermen on the dock last night, so people did fish around here.

Luke remembers it's Saturday. The beach will be crowded with bathers, not just fishermen. It's warm enough for swimming. In a couple of hours the place will be jammed with people.

The situation is still bad. He's thirsty and hungover. And there's a crust of sand over his lips. Fortunately, he can reach his face with his free left hand; just barely, but enough to wipe the grit away.

As long as he doesn't try to move, the pain in his body is more of a dull ache, secondary now to the stillness of his confinement. At least he doesn't feel the wetness of blood.

Unlike paralysis, in which the limbs are deadened, every inch of Luke's body is alive. His bones and flesh are held fast, but his nerves twist and turn, veering and leaping in all directions, trying to move until the agony bursts from his brain and Luke screams. Sound is his only freedom and he puts every fiber of power into the cry. It is so loud and long that there is even time to detach himself and listen. He's never heard that sound before. Not from anyone.

Except for the gentle splash of water lapping against the shore and distant seagulls, the answer is only silence.

Luke's energy dissipates; he lies quietly, exhausted and defeated. But only momentarily. Then the life force sweeps back in. Someone will come, he tells himself. Someone will come soon.

He closes his eyes to wait in the safety of darkness, hoping for sleep.

\* \* \*

Something touches Luke's cheek, waking him abruptly from his dreams. Instinctively, he shakes it off and opens his eyes. Inches from the left side of his face is the large furry head of a sheepdog. Luke turns aside and the dog begins to lick his ear with its pink tongue.

"Cut it out! Stop it!" Luke shoves the dog away with his head. But the dog persists and Luke shakes his head back and forth quickly in an effort to get out of the way. The dog likes the game; he pulls back on his feet with little yelps of pleasure then dives in again, aiming for Luke's ear.

Luke tries to swat him with his free arm but because he has to turn it backward, he doesn't have the power to push the big dog away. He keeps shaking his head, hoping the dog will get discouraged.

It doesn't really matter. Luke is overjoyed. The dog means there is a human in the vicinity. He's saved. It makes him feel good enough to smile at the big, dumb animal, who is waiting for the chance to jump in and lick him again.

Luke begins to shout, "Help! Help! I'm trapped in the sewer! Hello! Help me!"

The dog is stunned and pulls back, his tail sliding down between his legs as if he were being reprimanded. He starts to back away, edging toward the opening of the sewer.

"It's okay, boy. It's okay, come here. C'mon, boy, c'mon." Luke calls the dog in his friendliest voice, even smiles to make it more welcoming.

But the dog is nervous. He doesn't like being yelled at. It frightens him. He stands at the entrance for another instant and then suddenly, as if he had heard a whistle, he snaps his head up and listens. Waiting. An instant later, he bolts.

Luke shouts after him, "Come back! Help! Help!"

He doesn't stop yelling and shouting for many minutes. His

throat is raw and burning. After a couple of minutes, he calls out again.

And he waits. And waits.

No one comes. The dog whistle must have been from so far away only the sharp ears of an animal could have heard it. Too much of a distance for anyone to hear Luke's shouts, shouts that were mostly sucked into the depths of the tunnel to meet the echo.

Still, it's only a matter of time now. People *do* use the beach, they walk their dogs and fish and swim and …

That's when Luke remembers the sign about the beach being closed for renovations. Last night it was welcome. He and Daisy needed the privacy. Today …

No, he isn't worried. Nobody pays attention to those signs. He and Daisy didn't. And even if the regular people don't come, at least the workers will. They probably start early, maybe eight or so. Luke figures it's near seven o'clock by now.

It takes a little more figuring to realize that it's Saturday. There won't be any workers.

Weird calamities like this only happen to other people. It's a paragraph at the bottom of an unimportant page in a newspaper. Man trapped in rain sewer under a hundred pounds of beams and assorted shit. It doesn't say about the terror or the pain, how everything hurts.

To bring absolute reality to it, the most intense pain is the one he's brought on himself: a hangover the size of his own dear Australia that burns against his eyeballs with thumping spasms. Each pull feels like his brain is being ripped from his skull. On top of that is his nearly intolerable thirst.

When Luke finishes his litany of complaints he latches on to the best possibility: it's all a dream. He's going to wake up.

When that possibility is quickly exhausted—you don't *feel*

in a dream—there's always the silver linings: the rescue. Anybody but the police. Actually, even they wouldn't be a problem. He'd just say he'd been trapped for a couple of hours. No big deal. He'd give them his new name.

Still it would be better if the police didn't find him. Maybe a fisherman or a dog walker or—Daisy.

Daisy …

Even under these miserable circumstances, the thought of Daisy is surprisingly pleasant; better than that, exciting.

What would his friend Hank think of Daisy? So what, he's never going to meet her. Maybe Luke'll never see her again either. She said those kids knew her. Not good in a small town like this.

Just the thought of his best friend is enough to make his misery even worse. Incredible how he manages to screw up even the best things in his life.

Hank. He and Luke had only known each other for a couple of years, but the friendship started strong and stayed that way. It had happened fast, too, practically right from the first time they met at Shorty's bar in Century City.

It was afternoon. Luke was waiting around for an audition for yet another part he didn't get. Hank was just killing time between the matinee and evening performances at the Shubert Theater a few blocks away where he was working as an assistant stage manager. Had been for three years but now, he said, a small theater in Pomona was offering him full stage manager. He was probably going to take it. His real ambition was to be a director, and this would be a good start.

They started out bullshitting, bar talk, but right away they were comfortable. Luke remembers how they had talked for at least two hours, just the two of them. Then Hank had to go to the head and Luke was standing there alone and he looked around and realized that he'd been so involved in his conversation that he hadn't even seen how crowded the bar had gotten.

It was just like meeting a woman you were attracted to for the first time with a million words exploding out of you.

From there on, they became best friends, buddies, talking on the phone every day. They saw each other at least four times a week. Hank was the only real friend Luke had made since coming to the States. They had the same sense of humor and loved the set-up stuff. The scam game—not for money, just for the hell of it. To see how outrageous they could be. It was amazing where you could take ordinary regular people. And it was easy. If you stayed normal, you could be wildly ludicrous.

Being with Hank was the best part of Luke's time in LA. Nothing else worked like those little scenarios in the bar. They'd do a variation on the Lazarillo de Tormes tales. Hank introduced Luke to the Spanish short stories of the cruel master and miserable servant. Of course, with Hank directing. Only this time they were brothers, but like the sixteenth-century stories, the cruel master, Luke, would be blind. Hank played the perfect servant, groveling, toadying, finally annoying. Once they got the other bar patrons into the stream of their trust they could easily manipulate them. With a little imagination, it was a lesson on the human condition. Or an Arthur Miller playwriting course.

From the first, all the sympathy would go to Luke. Everyone went out of his way to make the blind man comfortable. But Luke's cruelty to his brother began to make them uneasy. Luke liked to watch how long it took them to turn. In the beginning they would try to laugh it off, give a little leeway to the handicapped. Then Luke would step up the cruelty until he felt their mood shift. When they soured enough, he would reinforce it, telling a little of Hank's background. How Hank had never worked a day in his life. All he did was lie around the house until their father threw him out. He landed in the gutter and that's where he'd lived for five years. Dirty, smelly, too lazy to even collect cans.

Despite the fact that Hank was neatly dressed in jeans and a clean T-shirt, his supporters would begin to edge away as if he still carried the stench of encrusted filth from the street. All pity vanished. A criminal couldn't have repelled them more.

How easy it was to take away someone's humanity, Luke thought. No wonder societies could be so easily manipulated.

Somebody once told Luke he should take acting lessons because he had the looks for Hollywood. Why would he need lessons if he could fool real people into thinking he was blind? Hell, he could do it for a whole afternoon without a script. In fact, that was what killed his acting, things like scripts and preparation, artificiality. Luke could only act if it was real.

Hank said there were teachers who worked like that, reality based. He was going to ask around and find one. Being a stage manager, he worked with actors all the time, often reading with them when they auditioned. He knew what he was talking about. Maybe that would have been the answer for Luke.

What the hell, it didn't matter now; he'd never see Hank again. Hank would never *want* to see him. That was the worst part—screwing his best friend over. It wasn't just the betrayal. Hank could lose all the collateral he'd put up to make Luke's bail. His car, maybe even his condo.

Yeah, but one day, Luke would make it all up to him. As soon as he got some money, the first thing he would do was pay back every penny Hank had spent. And more.

Christ, he'd had no choice but to jump bail. Well, technically he hadn't yet jumped because the trial date wasn't until July 17 and this was only what? The first? Still, by even leaving the state, he was in violation. But it didn't matter; there was no way he was going back to California.

By now, of course, Hank would know. Soon as he called and found out Luke's phone went straight to voicemail he would figure out that he jumped bail. Luke couldn't bear to think of how Hank would take it.

Maybe Hank would understand. He knew better than anyone that it was just a bad-luck accident. Actually, it was the other guy's fault. Luke was acting in self-defense. The guy had a knife. What was he supposed to do?

Okay, yeah, they'd pulled the bar trick on that guy. It wasn't just Luke; Hank was in on it too. It was so fucking harmless. Besides, the penalty for fooling somebody isn't supposed to be getting arrested. It's just a joke, but that dumb son-of-a-bitch with the knife who followed them out of the bar didn't get it.

On his own, the guy wasn't such a danger. He was actually shorter than Luke and kind of slight, but he was in a rage and coming at Luke with a knife. Luke was never looking for a fight; what he did was pure self-defense. He just kicked, not even a real kick, more like a shove with his foot. Didn't even touch the guy with his fist. The guy went down, tripping over his own foot. Funny, Luke had almost reached out to grab him.

But he didn't. And the guy fell backward. Before he could hit the ground, his head smashed into the top of a fire hydrant.

If only Luke had reached out and caught him. Luke was always the kind of person who would help if someone fell or needed assistance crossing the street; it felt natural to respond.

Maybe that was Australian, or just small town. And this time he was close enough to have grabbed the front of the guy's shirt and pulled him back. That's all it would have taken. That small move, a split second, and the guy would be fine. It would be nothing. How can such a crucial difference be so small, a little twist one way or the other? Except, maybe it wouldn't have been so fine if he had grabbed him; maybe it could have been Luke in the coma.

Still, if only he had trusted his first instinct and grabbed him ...

It all happened in less than a minute, there on the street in front of the bar. A million people around, then nobody. Nobody except that one woman, and she saw it all, but by the time the police and the ambulance came she'd disappeared. Hank had asked her what her name was, but later when they tried to look for her, they couldn't find her. It was probably a phony name. Like most people, she just didn't want to be involved. But if she knew how important it was ...

Hank said not to worry, that the police would find her, but Luke wasn't going to gamble on it. Of course, Hank was a witness, but he was also a friend. A good friend, the kind who'd put up bail for you. The kind who'd lie for you.

And then later what would happen when the police got around to the guys in the bar? They'd all say that Luke and Hank, both of them, were liars. Try to tell a jury it was just for fun. Just a playwriting experiment. Additionally, he'd overstayed his visa by like two years. Not good.

No, there was no way Luke could take that chance. Now it was an assault charge, but even if the guy died, it wouldn't be murder, it would be an involuntary manslaughter charge. And only the other guy's prints were on the knife. That would show if it wasn't an accident, it was self-defense. Still, you never knew what could happen.

Maybe the guy's family would get some hotshot lawyer. Maybe

they'd never find the female witness. Maybe, maybe, maybe. There were crazy things out there waiting to happen. Luke wasn't going to take the chance of hitting his own head on a fucking fire hydrant. He wasn't going to put his life on the line for another crazy shot out of the blue. So as soon as Hank bailed him out, Luke disappeared, headed straight for New York. A city you could get lost in.

But only if you don't fall asleep in a goddamn truck full of seafood and lose everything you own and then get yourself trapped in a rain sewer.

Jesus, how the hell did he get into this stupid situation? If it wasn't so tragic and didn't hurt so much, it would be laughable.

As long as he doesn't move, the pain in Luke's body is beginning to abate, lowering into achiness, although his head is still pounding. The familiarity of the hangover keeps things in perspective.

Just then he catches sight of two men. He has to twist his head to see around the side of the beam. But there they are, wearing T-shirts and jeans, no fishing poles, just standing at the water's edge right in front of him. In front of him—but maybe fifty feet away and facing the water.

"Hello! Help! Help!" Luke shouts. "Over here! In the sewer!" Why the hell don't they turn?

Could the tunnel be muffling his cries? He keeps shouting as loud as he can, but still they don't turn. They're talking, the two guys. In fact, from their body language and the fury with which they're nodding and shaking their heads, they could be arguing. Sons of bitches, they're so caught up in their own crap they aren't even paying attention to his cries.

"Help! Help! I'm trapped! I'm dying!"

Still, they don't turn. What the hell is the matter with them? Luke keeps shouting. Suddenly one man turns.

Thank God!

And looks right in his direction. "Help! Help! Over here!"

Then the other one turns. And the first one says something. With his hands. And the other signs his answer. And then they go back to their conversation, cooled down now, as they begin to walk down the beach in the other direction.

No!

"Are you friggin' deaf?" Luke screams after them.

Fuck! Now he has to pee. The idea of pissing himself changes everything. Trapped in a rain sewer—that has a certain romance to it. Pissing yourself turns it into something ugly, like a homeless bum on the street. Like the character Hank played in the bar.

The shame is too great. He'll have to hold it in until someone finds him, until he can stand up and piss like a man.

Judging from the time that has passed since dawn, Luke figures it's about eight or nine o'clock. The sun isn't sharp enough for him to read the angle and unfortunately his watch is on his right wrist, the one pinned under the wood. That'll teach him. Why doesn't he wear his watch on his left hand like everyone else? Years ago, when he got his first watch, his left wrist was in a cast from a bike accident. Who knew one day it was going to matter so much.

He can see it isn't going to be a great day weather-wise. In fact, it looks like it could rain. That wouldn't be good for Luke. People don't walk on the beach in the rain.

What the hell, though? Somebody has to come. People are everywhere. Hardly any empty places left. Go try to find a deserted beach to fuck on. Next thing you know, a bunch of kids will be pelting you with stones.

Someone has to come soon. Soon.

Luke's head still hurts but even that begins to quiet down. He could almost sleep if he didn't have to pee so badly. If someone doesn't come soon, he'll be out of luck.

The thought makes him smile. Beautiful; a guy trapped under all this shit worrying about being out of luck. How much more out of luck could he be?

When he thinks of luck, an image of Daisy flashes through his mind. Meeting Daisy, that was lucky.

Then the thunder comes, a loud clap followed by a bolt of lightning streaking across what Luke can see of the sky. At least he's out of the rain.

Another roar of thunder and more flashes of lightning. The drops begin to fall. The heavy raindrops fall straight down, each making a small plop as it hits the sand.

In no more than a moment, Luke becomes aware of water touching his right arm, the one pinned to the ground by the beam. Another instant and the water moves past his arms, wetting the sides of his face.

What the hell?

Almost instantly the sewer is running with nearly half a foot of water. As the current gets stronger, it picks up small pieces of stones and shells that graze Luke's body.

A rain sewer can run for miles and collect water as fast as it falls, sending it rushing toward the sea. In this case, toward the bay off Shorelane, Long Island.

Quickly, Luke realizes both the danger and the potential advantage. The water will lighten the weight of the wood and cement and give him a chance to free himself.

The danger: it could just as easily drown him.

The thought of such a death puts Luke into a frenzy. He struggles to wrestle his arms and legs out from under the accumulation, but most of the pile is above the water level and no lighter than before. Only his body is low enough to be immersed in the water. The weight of the fallen debris digs him into the sand, making him lower than the surrounding ground. The water begins to form a pool around him. Luke's folded jacket sweeps away, riding the bubbles of foam; the empty space under his head fills with water.

Panic leaves Luke gasping for breath. In order to keep his nose and mouth free, he has to keep his head bent backward and his chin as high as possible, putting his forehead underwater.

And no matter how he struggles, the current only grows stronger. The rainwater is now a rushing river. Luke's shoes slide off and sail down to the sea like little boats.

With his eyes underwater, Luke doesn't see the surge in the river; a wave rushes over his face, catching him in the middle of a breath and sending water up his nose. His head shoots up to reach for air but the water is too high. Luke's free arm waves back and forth desperately. Again, he reaches up with his head and this time breaks through the surface, sputtering and coughing and frantically sucking at the air.

Then, fast as it started, the downpour stops. Almost instantly, the water level drops. Within moments, it's down to a trickle.

Luke can't catch his breath or stop the wracking coughs. Each time he coughs, his head shoots up with such force that he expects his neck to snap. Finally, he gathers enough strength to vomit up the water and clear his lungs.

Without the jacket to hold up his head he has to stretch his neck back and rest his head uncomfortably on the sand.

"Oh, God, oh please, God, help me."

The water has gone and the immediate danger has passed, but nothing has changed. Luke's still trapped—only now he knows the true danger of his situation. Somebody has to get him out of there before it rains again. That little storm couldn't have been longer than five minutes. Not even. It was a shower. And yet, another minute of it and he would have drowned.

Suddenly he is overcome, not just with fear and the pain but with sadness. To add to the shame, he realizes that he's urinated. Like peeing in a pool with all that water, but still …

Tears fill Luke's eyes and overflow from the corners in a line down to his ears. Soft sobs escape him.

He's alone and he's going to die. Like maybe the guy outside the bar will. Then they'll both be dead, and it doesn't matter that neither of them deserved it. Sneaky, two deaths in one week posing as accidents. The LA guy's bashed skull happened fast, but Luke's is slow motion. And he has no way to stop it.

It's over. Everything. Every chance that had been available to him, every chance that he'd never taken. Every effort he'd never made. Always taking the easiest way, the one you never had to work for, or study for. How could he have wasted all those possibilities? And now, it was over. No more chances. There'd never even be a Daisy. Of all the regrets he could have, he's surprised how much that one hurts, this woman he'd only known for a couple hours. The pain of that imagined loss surprises him.

The sobs grow louder. Luke hears himself and part of him winces; the sounds are foolish, sounds no man would make. But the trauma of near death and the utter hopelessness of his situation rob him of the energy to stop.

Luke cries until he collapses into an exhausted sleep.

# CHAPTER TWELVE

Luke opens his eyes, looks up, and smiles though the pain. Saved.

Okay, it isn't Daisy; it's a bunch of kids. But they are wonderful, beautiful kids.

Hold the tragedy.

"Hey, am I glad to see you guys."

They're standing above him, so close they look ten feet tall. He can't tell how many they are but it looks like enough to do the job. They're boys; that helps.

"First thing you gotta do is get this stuff off me. It's heavy, but you can do it. I'll show you. C'mon, a couple of you guys grab the far end of the beam and the rest stay on this side. Okay?"

No one moves. They just stand, staring down at Luke.

"It's simple," Luke says, pointing with his free left hand. "Listen, you two go down near my feet and ..." He points again. "You guys stay up here. Got it?"

Still no one moves.

"C'mon, what are you waiting for?"

The three boys nearest him turn toward a fourth, half-hidden by the beam. Luke twists his head to see who they're looking at.

Shit, it's that fat kid from the store. The little bastard who was throwing stones last night. When he gets out of this mess, Luke's going to wring his friggin' little neck.

"Look," he tries to screw his face into a pleasant expression. "It's okay. I'm willing to forget about last night. Just help me get out of here, and we'll call it a day. Okay, kids?"

But Larry, the hefty one, bigger by a foot than the others, just shakes his head, no. No one else moves.

"Look, kids, this isn't a game. This is serious business. I'm hurt. You gotta help me."

"Homeless people are bums," Larry says.

"That's not nice to say, uh, what's your name?"

"His name's Larry," says the curly red-haired boy standing next to Luke's head.

"Larry. Didn't your mom teach you to respect your elders?"

"My ma says a bum'll steal the eyes out of your head. She says you guys steal from poor boxes."

"Well," says Luke, "you tell your ma I never stole anything in my life."

"Yeah, right," Larry laughs, looking around at his cohorts. "What about at Smilers?"

On signal from their leader, the other kids laugh and nod their heads. "Yeah, right."

"Hey, look, I'm not going to argue with you. Just get me out of here—help me free my arm."

They all look at Larry. He shakes his head. "Screw your arm."

"Kid, listen. People are going to be looking for me. You're all going to get in big trouble."

"Nobody's looking for you," Larry says. "Except maybe the police."

He laughs at his own joke and the others follow, slapping each other's shoulders like it's the funniest thing they've ever heard.

"Let me explain this to you, kid ... Larry." Luke speaks in a very calm adult voice, trying to distance himself from the children. "A little while ago it rained. No big deal, right? Just a few drops. Well, I almost drowned. All you need is a quick shower and in two seconds this goddamn sewer is full of water. You get that? I almost drowned. Now stop fooling around and get me out of here."

Larry smiles.

"My pa says we're in the middle of a drought. It's not going to rain for a couple weeks."

The other boy, Charley, the red-haired one standing near Luke's head, nods. "That's what my dad said, too."

The two other boys, who are twins who don't look at all alike, nod vigorously. "Yeah, right."

"Okay, maybe your dads are all right, maybe there won't be any big rain, but all you need is one freak storm and I drown. Understand?"

"There ain't gonna be one," Larry says. "My pa said."

"Your pa don't know beans. What the hell is he, a weatherman? What does he do anyway?"

"None of your business."

"He works for a cesspool company," Charley says.

"Shut up, Charley!"

"I was just saying what he does. I didn't mean anything," Charley mumbles apologetically.

Dennis Duncan leaps in. "It's none of your business, Charley." His twin, Benny, nods again, head bobbing idiotically.

"Oh Christ!" Luke can't believe what he's hearing. "Shut up, all of you! I don't give a shit what his father does. Just get me out of here!"

"We'll see," Larry says.

"What the hell does that mean?"

A little face ringed with the same curly red hair as Charley pushes through alongside Charley's legs. It's a girl, a pretty child, younger than the others. She looks down at Luke and there is something in her large brown eyes that is different from the boys. Confidence, but more than that, a stubborn set to her gaze. Whenever the boys speak they jerk their heads toward Larry. Checking his reaction. But the little girl looks straight at Luke.

"Everybody knows that when your mommy says, 'We'll see,' she means no."

"Mind your own business, Lucy," Larry says. "Hey, Charley, how come you let your sister talk to bums?"

"Yeah, Charley!" As always, Dennis is ready to jump on Larry's side. "Can't ya tell a homeless when you see one?"

And Benny follows, adding, "Can't ya?"

Lucy gives Benny a disgusted look and disappears behind Charley.

"First of all," Luke says, "You've got it wrong. I'm not a bum or a homeless person. Look, kids, I wasn't going to tell you this. I'm really not supposed to ..."

Luke sees that the possibility of a secret has grabbed their attention. He's on the right track. He's being Luke. He's in the bar. Whatever he's got to say to get out, he'll say.

"This has to stay very quiet. What do you say, guys, can I trust you?"

They all nod, even Larry.

"Where's the little girl, uh … Lucy, right?" Charley grabs his sister and shoves her up front.

"You too," Luke says, pointing at Lucy. "You gotta swear."

She doesn't answer. Just stares at him. The stubbornness really shows. But he isn't going to waste time trying to get her to agree. Even now, Luke isn't sure what he's going to say, but it has to be something that will get their respect. Something strong enough to get their obedience.

Then it comes to him. If he just relaxes, it always does. "You ever hear of the CIA?"

They snap up, eyes widening, all ears. He has them. Those bars in LA, the bullshit he and his friend, Hank, pulled with the grown men, that was hard stuff. This is like taking candy from a baby.

"I'm an undercover agent."

They actually say, "Wow!" All except Lucy and Larry. But he can see that Larry is buying it. Lucy, he's not so sure about.

"I've been with the agency for eight years. Normally, I work overseas because I'm fluent in six languages. *Haim hors vishon an dis.* You know what that is?"

They all shake their heads.

"Arabic. My Japanese is very rusty. I haven't been there in years, but my Russian is perfect. What's your name, kid?" he says, pointing to the white-haired twin.

Benny looks at Larry for permission, but Larry just shrugs his shoulders.

So he tells him, "Benny."

"Do you know how to say 'My name is Benny' in Russian?"

Benny shakes his head, no.

"*Goshondi vaco Benja.*" Luke gives them two more made-up phrases in no discernible language. They're all impressed except

Lucy, who keeps the impassive look on her face. For some reason, Luke worries that she might know he's full of shit, but it's impossible; she's just a little kid. He goes on.

"You've got some laboratories out here in Shorelane that even the people who live here aren't aware of. Any place where there's secret work going on, you have to be very careful. There are spies all around. You know those people who own the bookstore in town?" Yesterday, Luke had passed a bookstore on the way to Smilers.

"The Ruddermans?" Charley says, genuinely surprised.

"Yeah, that's them. That's why I'm here."

"But they're old," Benny says, "and they were here when my parents were little kids. They even had the same store."

"That's right. They've been eluding us for years. And doing terrible damage. We gotta stop them."

"Are you going to kill them?" Charley asks.

"You can't ask me that," Luke says. "In fact, don't ask me any more questions. I've already said too much."

"How do we know you're not the spy?" Larry asks.

"I just told you." It's hard to keep an even tone with Larry; Luke wants to get up and slap him in the face. He's like every bully Luke has ever known. He remembers Bebrey, whose house he had to pass every day on the way to school when he was little. Bebrey was a mean kid who only hung around with little kids so he could bully them. A lot like Larry.

"I think you're the enemy spy," Larry says. The others begin to nod their heads. "Yeah, maybe he's even in with the Ruddermans. My pa don't like them anyway. They're Jews, ya know."

Lucy looks up at her brother. Charley swallows hard and looks away.

"Hey, Chucko," Larry says, "I know you're Jewish, but they're foreign Jews. That's different, right?"

Charley shrugs his shoulders. "I guess …"

"Jesus, Charley," Luke says. "You gonna let him say that?"

"Shut up, spy." Larry pokes Luke with a branch he's found on the ground.

"You better be careful, Larry, you don't want to mess with the CIA." Luke pretends not to notice the poke.

"There's probably a reward for this guy. Maybe a hundred thousand dollars," Larry says, poking him again. Harder.

"Cut it out," Luke says.

"Make me, spy," Larry says, shoving the stick into Luke's bare foot. He hands the stick to Benny. "Go on, poke his leg."

Without hesitation, Benny takes the stick and does as he's told, sticking it into Luke's shin hard enough to draw blood. Now Dennis grabs the stick and is about to poke Luke's leg when Luke shouts, "Stop this! What the hell are you doing?"

Dennis looks over at Larry who nods his head. And Dennis pokes Luke's thigh, two, three, four times, cutting thin lines that turn red with blood. Then he hands the stick to Charley.

Luke looks up at the curly-haired boy and shakes his head, "Don't do it. You know it's not right."

"You gonna listen to an enemy spy over me?" There's a threat in Larry's voice, and even that small edge is enough to convince Charley to do what he's told. He takes the stick and tentatively touches it to Luke's arm.

"What are you doing, tickling him? Give him a good shove. Even if this guy's not a spy, he's a bum." Larry is angry now. "Remember what he did to us in the store?"

"Don't do it!" Luke puts as much threat as he can in his voice, but he can't match the bully's control. Charley shoves him hard.

"You little bastard!" Luke grabs Charley's ankle with his free left hand and holds on tight as Charley screams in terror. Cursing, Larry grabs the stick and begins to beat Luke's arm while the other boys kick and punch at the trapped man. Lucy has her brother's arm, struggling to pull him out of Luke's grasp.

Then Larry starts to whack at Luke's face with the stick, long high slashes that sing through the air. The stick bites into Luke's skin, slicing his forehead, cutting his cheeks, narrowly missing his eyes.

Instantly, Luke lets go of Charley's ankle, but Larry doesn't stop pounding on him, now his chest, now his arms. The other children stare in horrified fascination, stunned, listening to Luke's screams as Larry, grunting with every swing, loses himself in the beating.

That's when Lucy, the only child who hasn't scrambled back against the wall, tugs hard at Larry's shirt. It breaks his trance and the bully stops, looking down at the little girl. He twists his arms and holds the stick poised in the air over her head. She stands frozen in terror; quickly, Charley reaches out and grabs her arm, pulling her back away from Larry.

"Jesus Christ!" Luke's voice quivers with pain and fright. "What are you doing? You want to kill me?" And then unashamedly pleading: "What's the matter with you kids? What did I ever do to you? For Christ's sake ..."

"Told you he was dangerous," Larry says, struggling to catch his breath and bring control to his shaking body. "If I hadn't hit him, he would've broken Charley's ankle. He's a killer."

"What are you talking about? I never hurt anyone in my life."

Benny is safely away from Luke and can be bold. "Yeah, well, you said you were CIA. They kill, right, Larry?"

All the boys, including Larry, nod. Lucy just watches.

"Everybody knows the CIA kills anybody who gets in their way. They probably kill millions of people every day," Larry sneers.

Luke makes a last desperate attempt. "I work in the office. I don't know anything about killing people."

But Larry has an answer for that, too. "You tell them who to kill."

"I never did." Realizing he's facing an argumentative dead end, Luke takes a deep breath and speaks in his most reasonable voice. "Okay. Maybe I wasn't really in the CIA …"

"You lied?" Larry sounds shocked.

"Yeah, I lied. It was just a story I thought you kids would like. I'm a regular guy. I'm only passing though Shorelane on my way to the Hamptons."

"See, I told you," Larry says. "He's a bum."

"I'm not a bum. And anyway, that's not important now," Luke says. "What's important is to get me out. I'm sorry if I scared you …"

"I wasn't scared," Charley says, "I was just surprised, right, Larry?"

"Whatever," Luke says, smiling apologetically. "I'm sorry for taking you by surprise, Charley, but this has been very terrible for me. Can you find something to put under my head? My neck is killing me. It was that cement stuff on the ceiling there. It must have come loose when the train went by. See up there?" He points with his left hand to what was left of the shoring. "See?"

Luke turns his head to look at the kids. But they're gone.

He calls, "Larry! Charley! Kids! Come back! I gotta get out of here. I need water. For Christ's sake, help!"

Outside of his echo, there's no response. The children have disappeared. Surely they're going for help. Even little shits wouldn't just let someone die.

Would they?

# CHAPTER THIRTEEN

The children aren't far, just outside the sewer entrance, but to the side where Luke can't see them. They hear him calling, but Larry shakes his head; don't answer.

"What are we gonna do?" Charley whispers.

"We're gonna do what I say, that's what."

"So what do you say, huh, Lar?" Benny asks.

"Yeah, what are we gonna do with him?" Dennis is always right behind his twin.

"So what'd I say?"

The other kids shrug uncomfortably.

"Right, assholes, I didn't say nothing. When I do, you'll know it." Larry always seems so smart and controlled, like he knows everything. At least that's what it looks like to the twins. Charley is just afraid of him.

"Hey," Larry calls in a loud whisper to Lucy.

Charley turns to see his sister dragging a gallon jug of water toward the sewer entrance.

"Come here." Angry, Larry motions toward himself.

She stops, but she doesn't come toward him. "He said he needed water," she says.

"Get that water," Larry tells Charley. Charley immediately grabs the jug out of Lucy's hand. She doesn't fight him. She doesn't say anything, just lets go.

"Put it over there," Larry orders, pointing to a clump of grass. "You know, your sister's a pain in the ass. Can't you ever leave her home? Just tell 'em you don't wanna bring her. Or maybe you should stay home."

"Yeah," the twins say in unison.

"Shut up, assholes." Charley turns on them. Then to Larry, "I'm talking to my parents tonight. I'm telling them they gotta get someone to watch her or something."

Larry is always saying Charley should leave Lucy at home. And Charley is always saying he's going to talk to his parents. Nothing Charley would like better than to leave her home. So what if his parents have to work? He'll help pay for a babysitter with some money out of his allowance. He's going to tell them no ten-year-old boy should have to drag his seven-year-old sister everywhere.

What's really bad is having Lucy see him with Larry. She has to know how scared he is. She never says anything, but he knows she knows.

She's a weird kid. Always watching. Really smart, but really quiet. And she doesn't look like she's afraid of anything. She's only a girl and she's little and anybody could push her around. Except they don't. Something about her makes people not even try.

Charley secretly wishes he could be more like her.

"Okay," Larry says, "let's get out of here. We're gonna have a meeting and then I'm gonna say."

He starts over the dunes, the scraggly band following. They push down the plastic fence and run across the parking lot. Just then a passing police car slows, and the driver rolls down his window.

"Hey, you kids. Come over here!"

The children stop dead and look at Larry. This time he's scared too.

"Come here!" the cop repeats.

They stumble over to the police car. Somehow Dennis gets stuck in front. Charley takes Lucy's hand. Benny follows his brother and Larry manages to be last.

"Were you kids down on the beach?" the cop asks.

Every one of them, including Lucy, shakes their head, no. The cop knows they're lying. He warns them that it's dangerous with the construction, and if he finds out they were playing on the beach, he'll arrest them for trespassing. And that means their parents will have to pay a $500 fine. He looks right at Larry.

"I don't think your dad's gonna like that much, right, O'Neill?"

Larry doesn't answer, just nods in agreement. Any mention of his father gets his instant attention.

"You too, Duncans, and Charley, you better watch out bringing your little sister to a dangerous place like this."

The cop, Danny Dasto, is in his late thirties. He went to school with Larry's father, John O'Neill, and Charley's father, Ned Adler. Even if he hadn't, Shorelane is so small that everyone knows everyone else. A new cop would learn the kids' names in a week.

"Okay, now beat it, all of you. Why don't you go over to the playground on Cedar?"

Dismissed, they take off at top speed down the street. As soon as the cop car is out of sight, Larry stops.

"He's such an asshole. My dad hated him in school."

Charley doesn't say that Danny is a good friend of his father's. But Lucy does.

"Yeah, well, he's still an asshole. C'mon," Larry says, "let's go back to your house, Charley. I need some stuff."

Charley isn't supposed to bring friends to his house when his parents aren't home, but he can't say no to Larry.

# CHAPTER FOURTEEN

Luke watches the portion of the sky he can see begin to change. The pale sunlight fades, and though he can only see a thin strip of the water, he is aware that the color has turned from rich blue to steel gray. He can smell the threat of rain in the air, and the pain in his trapped arm is throbbing, and the cuts from that goddamn kid sting.

Every few minutes he shouts for help. He never gets an answer. The children have to come back. Or maybe they'll send someone else. Daisy said she knew them; maybe they'll find her. Larry would have a good time embarrassing her. That's a painful thought. Luke would like to kill the little bastard.

But whatever they decide, they won't just walk away and leave him. That would be unnatural. Luke understands they don't fully appreciate the urgency of his situation, but kids just don't do monstrous things like that, do they? Even a kid like Larry. Yeah, he's got a bad temper, but the others will stop him when he gets too crazy. Like that little girl did.

No, they'll definitely come back.

The day has turned decidedly gray now. Luke mustn't let himself panic.

He forces his mind to a safe place. What if he had never left Australia? Probably he would have ended up in the equivalent of a rain sewer, trapped under a wife, kids, and a no-place job. Dumb high school kid that he was, he knew not to take that chance; he knew there had to be more. What he didn't know was that you had to work for it.

He'd told people he was going to the States, that he'd been accepted at Yale. It gave him an excuse for the right kind of leaving, and everyone was happy for him. Even his mother seemed pleased. Why she bought the story he never understood; she had to have known better. But maybe she was ready to step out from under responsibility she never really wanted.

Or maybe she just wanted to get him out of her sight. Never have to look at those see-through blue eyes lined with thick lashes so dark they seemed to have nothing to do with his blond-streaked hair.

"Watery," she'd said about his eyes. "Like your father's."

Not that there were any pictures of his father around. Luke searched endlessly over the years, looking in every corner of the house, but he never found one. And while his mother was never overtly unkind—she was too meek for that—he knew she didn't like him.

She didn't like him because he was part of the man who had abandoned her.

But only he knew that. Anyone else would think she was simply a vague sort of woman. Not particularly interested in anything. Truth be told, Luke could never find her passion. Even her anger toward his father was passive. As passive as the emptiness she felt for her son.

Anything that Luke ever did wrong, even the most insignificant, was always compared to his father. From all the comments on their similarity, they might have been identical twins, not father and son.

Goin' nowhere, that's what she always said about him. That boy's goin' nowhere.

Most of the time, she only seemed vaguely aware of Luke's existence. When she wasn't working, she was home. She never left the house. Never took him to a movie or any place special other than necessary appointments like the dentist or doctor. No friends ever stopped in. Luke never knew his father or any family outside of her. She stopped talking to her own relatives before he was born. His memories of those years were of silence. Other than to tell Luke to make his bed or do some other chore, she never really spoke to him, and since no one came to the house, and they didn't have conversations, they could go for hours in silence.

One day, on his way home from school, he found an abandoned puppy. It didn't have a collar or a name tag, so he took him home, and surprisingly, his mother didn't object. He had Spotty, part dalmatian, and now he would have someone to talk to. And he did, and there was sound in the house, and it felt so good and normal, he thought maybe he could ask some friend from school to come over. He never had before because he thought his silent mother was too strange, and he didn't want anyone from school to see what it was like in his house.

But he never got the chance, because about three weeks later, he came home after school and Spotty was gone. He didn't want to, but he had to ask her what happened.

"He was too much trouble," she said. Nothing more.

He knew he hated her that day, but so what? It was too late for Spotty. And the house was silent again.

How different his life was going to be when he grew up and left the silent house, he used to think. Except it wasn't. It wasn't silent, but it was empty, and that's like a silence.

How different it would be if it were different. If he ever got out of here, he swore that whatever it took, he would make it different.

The one picture of his mother in the house was strange because it wasn't about an event, like a graduation or even wedding, it was just a headshot that sat in a silver frame on her night table. It showed a pretty, petite woman, too thin, with a prominent collarbone and flat breasts. As far back as he could remember, she'd had gray hair and pale brown eyes that stared into the middle distance. When he was a teenager, he decided she was waiting for his father to come home.

Waiting ... but not to welcome him with a kiss. Oh no. To kill him? Maybe. But if she did, it would be gentle, nothing violent. Poison. She wouldn't care what happened to herself afterward. Or to her son, the spawn of her lamentable mistake.

When Luke was little, he would ask about his father. She'd say simply that she didn't know him at all, but he looked exactly like Luke. She'd married a stranger, she told him. Without softening it up for a child, she said that the marriage had lasted less than a month. Luke's father had gone off, and she'd never heard from him again. And Luke would wonder, how do you know I do all the things like him if you only knew him for a few weeks?

She said Tom Schnekk, the name on his parents' marriage certificate, wasn't even his father's real name. Whoever he was, he probably didn't even know about Luke. At other times, his mother just wouldn't answer his questions at all. As he got older, he stopped asking.

In order to get a student visa, he had to enroll at the

University of Seattle. When he landed, even at the airport on that first day, he knew he was going to love the United States. Americans had good feelings about Australia; after an entire history of being looked down on by Europe, it offered another new world in which they could be equal. Everyone said Australia was like America had been in the thirties.

His newfound determination lasted less than a term. But school wasn't a waste. It led him to decide on his life's work, and the only preparation required was reading, one of his favorite pastimes.

Luke was going to be a writer. The choice didn't come out of the blue; he'd always had a natural writing style. Teachers encouraged him, but like with so many other things, he wouldn't put in the effort. Perhaps he worried he wouldn't be good enough. His mother would have agreed. Joining his high school newspaper or starting a blog felt like putting too much on the line. But now he'd pursue his talent. He'd do the work.

The memory brings him back to his present plight. You couldn't ask for a better story—providing it has a happy ending. That's why he needs the kids.

Just that thought makes Luke feel hopeful, and he thinks he sees a slight change in the light. It's gotten a tiny bit brighter.

Yes, it's definitely not as gray.

# CHAPTER FIFTEEN

The children walk toward the Adler house along the same route Luke and Daisy took the night before. As they approach Main Street, Larry sends Benny ahead to look for the cop car while the rest of them wait in the alley. Benny gives the all-clear, and cautiously they start across Main Street.

Suddenly, someone calls out Lucy's name.

The kids stop and turn in the direction of the voice. It's Daisy Rumkin, standing in front of Smilers. The boys look at Larry, but Larry is watching Lucy.

The girl hesitates then walks toward Daisy, who smiles at her. "Hi, Lucy. Can I talk to you for a minute, honey?"

Lucy nods, but doesn't speak or smile back. The boys are watching.

"I really feel bad about yesterday, and I wanted to explain."

Lucy likes Daisy. Her silence isn't born of hostility; she just doesn't know what Daisy is going to say, and she's afraid the grown-up will ask about Luke.

"Sweetie, it wasn't nice what Larry and the other boys did. That Larry's an awful little boy; you really shouldn't hang around with him. He's a bully."

Lucy nods.

Daisy goes on, "But that's not what I wanted to talk about. I'm real sorry what you had to see. I mean, with Luke and me. I guess it was dumb of me to do something like that in the open. I apologize, but the beach was supposed to be closed and we thought … Well, he's an old friend …"

Lucy's big brown eyes go wide.

Daisy wanted the conversation, had made up her mind to find Lucy, but now she doesn't know what to say. She certainly isn't going to tell Lucy that she just met Luke that afternoon. That was not the message you wanted to send a seven-year-old. So she stumbles around, searching for an explanation.

"I mean, once we were in love."

It's getting worse. The child still says nothing.

"Actually, we used to live together." There, that sounds better. Like marriage, but not.

"Here?" Lucy asks.

"No. Not exactly, well, not anymore. Actually, he never really lived here." Daisy is choking on her own lies. "But he's staying for a couple of days now."

"Here?" Lucy repeats, almost alarmed.

Larry and the other boys have crossed the street and are standing about twenty feet away. Watching Lucy's face, Larry's eyes narrow; he grabs Charley, twisting the smaller boy's arm.

"Go get your sister."

Charley hesitates. Larry shoves him in the back. "Now!"

Daisy wonders if she should tell Lucy about Luke being in the movies but decides that would be too confusing.

"Yes, honey, for a couple of days."

Lucy looks overwhelmed. She opens her mouth, takes a breath, and starts to speak—just as her brother grabs her arm.

"C'mon, Lucy. Mom's waiting."

Lucy turns to Charley. "Mom's not home."

"Yes, she is; she just got home. C'mon," he says, pulling her away from Daisy.

"Wait a minute, Charley," Daisy calls, but Charley isn't stopping for anyone. Not with Larry waiting and angry.

Daisy watches them go. Slowly, she points to Larry and calls out, "You better watch yourself."

He responds by giving her the finger. Daisy grimaces. Everyone hates that kid—though from what she's heard, nobody hates him *more* than his own father does.

That conversation with Lucy leaves Daisy more disturbed than ever. The child is obviously upset about what happened, and Daisy needs more time to explain things. She isn't going to chase after her though, not with the boys around. She'll wait until she can catch Lucy alone.

\* \* \*

As Lucy and Charley come near, Larry walks over and pushes Charley away from his sister. "C'mere," he says, pulling the little girl into the doorway of the shoe shop. "See this?" Surreptitiously, he slips a Swiss Army knife from his pants pocket and flips open a blade. "Stick your tongue out."

Lucy is frozen with fear.

"*Stick your tongue out*, I said."

There's such menace in Larry's voice that Lucy has no choice but to obey. With great reluctance she pushes the very tip of her tongue out so that it barely peeks between her lips, holds it for an instant, and pulls it back.

"You say anything to her or anybody else, and I'm gonna cut your tongue out. I'll make Benny and Dennis hold you down. Maybe I'll make Charley hold your mouth open. You got it?"

Lucy nods her head up and down, up and down.

"Not to your parents, not to nobody. You don't talk."

Lucy is still nodding.

The other children watch silently. Charley knows he would jump in there, throw his whole body against Larry, if he thought Lucy was really in danger. At least, that's what he tells himself. Besides, Larry was always doing that knife thing to scare the twins. Still, it was scary.

"I said nobody. Now swear," Larry says, grabbing Lucy by the bunched-up front of her T-shirt.

This time, Lucy is silent not from choice but from terror.

"Say it." Larry pokes her hard in the ribs, holding up the knife in front of her eyes.

"I swear."

Anyone but Lucy would be in tears. She's certainly frightened enough, but it's strange with Lucy; she doesn't talk much and she doesn't cry. Not often. When her grandmother died, she did. More than Charley. And when the girl next door accidentally slammed Lucy's little finger in the car door, then she cried. But those were rare times. Nobody could call Lucy Adler a crybaby.

"Let's go," Larry says.

Right now, Charley is working on another worry. What if his parents are home? But maybe that would be okay. In fact, it could be good because then he could dump Lucy. But they might want to know what was happening and where they were going and everything else parents always want to know. When they weren't home he could be doing anything, but they never ask about that. It's weird.

If they aren't home now but come home when all the kids are there, they would be angry. It's an absolute rule: no friends in the house when his parents aren't home.

He doesn't know whether he wants them to be home or not. Charley is a worrier.

# CHAPTER SIXTEEN

Charley didn't have to worry. His parents don't come home while they're all inside the house. The kids eat peanut butter sandwiches and drink Cokes. And they laugh about Luke, as they listen to the million wild plans Larry has for what to do with him.

Charley asks if maybe they should bring Luke something to eat. And that starts a whole hysterical menu thing, with Larry examining the contents of the refrigerator, pulling out one jar after another. "A pickle sandwich, a horseradish sandwich, left-over broccoli, an orange juice sandwich, an olive oil sandwich ..." On and on. "A puke sandwich, a snot sandwich ..." Every new suggestion is met with screams of laughter.

Well, not from Lucy. But everyone knows she doesn't have a sense of humor.

Finally, Larry himself makes Luke an ordinary peanut butter sandwich. But before he closes it, he sucks up the snot from his nose and spits in it. All the boys fall down laughing.

Then Larry compiles a list of things they need. Rope, he tells

Charley. Lucy keeps playing dumb about her jump rope, but Charley finds another piece of rope in the garage. Then Larry tells them to get some long poles. They settle on some extension curtain rods from the basement. While they're down there, Larry takes a wrench from Mr. Adler's toolbox and a can of white paint. Benny helps himself to the plastic cover from the barbecue, but Charley makes him put it back.

That's when Larry picks it up. He looks at Charley, who doesn't object, rolls it up, and hands it back to Benny.

"We gotta go," Charley says, his worrying in full bloom. "My parents are gonna be home any minute. Right, Luce?"

Lucy stands silently at the door, a small cushion tucked under her arm. She nods her head in agreement.

"What's that for?" Dennis asks, pointing to the cushion.

"It's mine," she answers.

It isn't ever worth messing with Lucy, so Dennis just mumbles, "Butthead," and looks at Larry.

"Let's go," Larry says.

"You go," Charley tells him, "I wanna lock up."

Larry walks out, the twins following. Charley frantically tries to clean up the remains of the lunch party.

Lucy waits for him.

# CHAPTER SEVENTEEN

Luke has never been as happy to see anybody in his whole life as he is to see those five children. He's a little disappointed that they haven't brought any adults but relieved and delighted that they came back.

Though the children keep their distance, he can see that they have bags of supplies. He guesses they've brought stuff to help lift the wood and cement.

And water, he prays.

Whatever problems he's had with them, he has to keep remembering that they're only children. Even if this isn't the best way, they're still trying to help. He can empathize; this has all the earmarks of an exciting adventure, and they probably want to play at being heroes.

He'll let them give it a try; if they can't move the cement, he'll send them for help.

"Hey kids, am I happy to see you. You didn't happen to bring any water, did you? I'm dying of thirst."

They didn't, but Benny remembers the gallon jug in the weeds. "Yeah, we found some outside," he says. "Should I get it, Lar?"

"Sure, get it."

Luke smiles. "Thanks, guys. My mouth feels like the inside of a motorman's boot." It's an old expression he's heard all his life. Personally, he never understood why a motorman's boots would be especially dry, but it sounds friendly and he wants to put the children at ease, show them there're no hard feelings.

They're good kids. He can see that the little girl has actually brought a cushion for his head.

"We brought you lunch," Dennis says.

"Great."

"A peanut butter sandwich," Larry says. "You like peanut butter?"

"Love it."

With the exception of Lucy, they all start laughing. In the spirit of camaraderie, Luke laughs too.

Benny comes back with the water, and then they have to figure out how to get it to Luke without getting too close. They're very wary of him since he grabbed Charley.

It's decided that Larry will push the jug over to Luke with the curtain rod, but the gallon jug is too heavy, and Larry can't keep it straight. After a few attempts, they manage to move it close enough to Luke's left hand for him to grab it. Now the problem is how he can get it to his mouth without spilling too much. It's almost full and very heavy.

The children watch as Luke uncaps the top, puts the cap on his chest, picks up the jug, raises his head as high as he can, and brings the water to his lips.

It pours out over his face, but he'd expected to lose at least a quarter because of the bad angle. As long as he's able to get enough liquid to quiet his raging thirst, it's okay.

It's a little annoying to have the children laughing at his clumsiness, but what the fuck, they did bring him the water.

"Hey, mister," Larry says, trying to hide a grin that keeps escaping at the sides of his mouth, "you ready for your lunch?"

"Sure, pass it over."

Again, the children use the rods to push the sandwich until Luke can reach it. Hungry as he is, the last thing he wants is peanut butter. But they're all waiting with such expectation that he can't disappoint them.

He unwraps the sandwich and takes out half. They watch him as if they've never seen anyone eat before. He'll give them their money's worth.

He takes a bite.

"Great! Thanks."

With the usual exception of Lucy, the four boys double over in glee, snorting with laughter, punching each other on the shoulders, behaving like little assholes.

Obviously Luke looked peculiar trying to reach the sandwich to his mouth. But not that funny.

He could learn to hate these children very easily. Okay, not Lucy, but the other four. Luke can remember being ten or eleven, but even then, he was never an asshole like these kids. He liked to think he had more backbone.

Strangely, he thinks he'd have been most like the little girl.

"Honey," he says gently to Lucy. "Did you bring that cushion for my head?"

She looks defiantly at Larry and her brother, and then nods.

"Could you just put it under my head? My neck is breaking from trying to hold it up."

Lucy moves toward Luke, but Charley pulls her back. "Lu, are you nuts? You get close enough and he's gonna grab you!"

"No," Luke says, "I swear I won't. I'm sorry, Charley, I just wanted you to listen to me. I didn't mean to scare you."

"Fuck you, you didn't scare me."

"I meant I didn't mean to hurt you."

"Fuck you, you didn't hurt me either."

"Okay, whatever. I can't lie here like this. Just shove the cushion over with the stick, all right?"

"Me, me," Dennis says, "I wanna do it." He takes the cushion from Lucy and starts pushing it toward Luke.

Then away from Luke.

"Hey, it don't like him. Look at that, it don't wanna go."

Now Benny takes his rod and shoves the cushion in the other direction, toward Luke. "Yes, it does. Hey, looka that!"

Larry gets into the act, pushing the cushion toward Benny. "It likes you, Benny."

"Hey, how about me?" Charley reaches out with his pole and pulls the cushion in. "It likes me."

Luke can do nothing but watch.

In an instant it becomes a free-for-all, rods and poles flying and banging, pounding on the cushion. Finally, Larry gets his pole under the cushion and sends it sailing through the air. It lands at Lucy's feet. Lucy scoops it up, runs over to Luke, and stuffs it under his head, then runs back to the sidelines where Larry grabs her arm hard, throwing her off balance.

"Who told you to do that?"

"She didn't mean anything," Charley answers. "She's always

doing things like that. Sometimes she doesn't hear so good, right?"

Lucy doesn't even look at her brother.

"See," he says, "she didn't hear me."

"Next time she does something like that, I'm gonna fuckin' make her hear me."

Lucy pulls on Charley's sleeve. "I have to pee."

"So go outside, near the weeds."

"No. I wanna go home."

"Yeah," Larry says. "Take the pain in the ass home."

"No, wait," says Luke. "We need Charley to help get me out."

"How do ya know we're gonna get you out?" Larry says.

Luke turns his head to look at Larry. Patience, he tells himself, stay adult. He pulls up a smile as if catching the joke. "Yeah right. Funny."

"I wanna go home now."

"Let's go, butthead." Charley walks toward the entrance to the sewer. Lucy is already out. "See ya."

And he's gone.

"What do ya wanna do, Larry?" Dennis asks.

Larry pays no attention. "You don't sound American," he says to Luke.

"I'm Australian. Like Mel Gibson."

"You know him?"

Suddenly, Luke feels he has a shot at making contact with Larry, but he has to play it carefully. "Not well. He's related to my uncle."

"No shit!" All three boys are impressed.

"Only by marriage." Even a distant relationship with a movie star would give Luke some standing. He can't be a homeless person if he's related to Mel Gibson. "I stayed with him in LA."

"Yeah, so what's his telephone number?" Larry is relentless and not stupid.

"I can't do that to him. You know stars don't give out their private numbers."

"Bullshit. You don't even know him."

"How about this? He was born in 1953 in Melbourne, Australia. Mother's maiden name Nora Henley; father Sam Gibson. His ex-wife is the former Sara Leight, and her father is my mother's uncle, David Leight. That good enough?"

"Wow!" says Benny. "He really knows him."

"Unless he's making it all up."

"Tell ya what," says Luke, stronger now. "Why don't you just look it up?"

"Where?"

Luke can see that Larry is going to challenge him on everything. He has to show conviction. Bullies like Larry are always on the lookout for weakness. You show weakness, he sinks his teeth in.

"Go home and google him," Luke says with just enough annoyance in his voice to show confidence.

"Okay," says Larry, "let's go home."

"Wait a minute!" Luke snaps. "How about getting me outta here first?"

"How about we check and see if you're a liar? If you are, then we'll know you're probably also a spy."

"Then we'll call the police," Dennis says.

"Great," says Luke. "Nothing I'd like better than for you to call the police. Surprised?" he says to Dennis. He has no trouble handling Dennis, his brother—even Charley. It's Larry. And now Larry's smiling.

"Let's test him," Larry says.

"Ask me any question you want."

"We're not gonna test you that way. I got another way. C'mon, guys."

"Where are you going? Come back. You gotta stop this fooling around and get me out of here!"

"Says who?" Larry keeps on walking.

Luke struggles to control his fury, but his teeth bare and an animal growl escapes his lips. If he could get his hands on that kid, he'd rip him apart. He's shocked to feel such rage and hate for a child, but underneath this ugly passion he's beginning to feel something even more frightening: a terrible emptiness, a total lack of power. How could this have happened? He's an adult, a man of substance …

But of course he isn't a man of substance. If he had been, no one, certainly not these children, could have disrespected him in such a manner.

*How do they know I'm not?* he asks himself. *What do they see?* Before he can answer, Larry and the twins come back. Benny and Dennis are each holding one side of a large bucket filled with water, probably lifted from the construction site. Luke can't help but think what a fuckin' lot of stupid giggling kids do. They can barely stand up straight for all their swallowed laughter, and each time they double over more water spills out of the bucket.

"Put it on this side," Larry says, pointing to a spot next to his feet. "Okay, now, Loki, you answer some questions and if you're right, we pull off some of the stuff."

"And if he's not?" Benny wants to know.

"Then we do the sandballs. You ready, Loki?"

"My name is Luke."

"Okay, Loki, first question. What is my mom's sister's name?"

All three, even Larry, collapse in gales of laughter. Luke makes no answer.

Larry counts, one one thousand, two one thousand, three one thousand, until he gets to ten.

Luke remains silent. There is a certain dignity to silence. It's what a man of substance would do.

"Okay, let 'er go!" Larry says, and sends a gritty ball of sand and water right at Luke's exposed arm. It hits his forearm, splattering him with wet sand.

Now Dennis asks his question. "What is my aunt Sarah's name?"

"Asshole!" Larry says.

"What?"

"You already said."

"I didn't."

"Tell him, Benny."

And he tells him and Dennis says he meant his other aunt and that starts an argument between the brothers and all the while Luke is silent.

"Fuck the game," says Larry. "Let's just aim and you gotta say first where and then if you hit where you said you get a point. First one with five points wins."

The children dip sand into the bucket and line the balls up at their feet. When they've made ten each, they call out where they're aiming and start throwing.

Luke the target has nothing to do with Luke the human being.

Luke flinches when the balls hit his face but otherwise shows no reaction. What is there about him that allows these children to take such liberties? He isn't deformed, disfigured, or mentally disadvantaged, the kind of person children traditionally pick on ... But whatever his vulnerability, they sense it. If he can't count on the normal respect children have for their elders, he has to find something else.

Another ball hits his forehead and the sand crumbles in his eyes. Rather than wipe it with his free hand, he keeps his eyes shut and doesn't move.

If the kids notice his lack of response, they give no indication. In fact, if anything, the game becomes more intense. Benny is foolish enough to be beating Larry. Luke knows Larry will end the game before Benny can win. And indeed, just as Benny is about to throw for his fifth hit, Larry dumps the bucket of water over his head.

"Hey! Whaddya doin'?" Benny says, jumping back.

"Fuckin' cheater!" Larry leaps at Benny, knocking him down, pummeling him with his fists. Dennis's natural instinct to help his brother pulls at him hard, but still he can only stand in terror as Larry bloodies the smaller boy, pounding his head against the rocky sand, screaming over and over, "Fuckin' moron! Fuckin' cheater!"

"Stop him! For Christ's sake, stop him!" Luke shouts to Dennis. "Make him stop!"

But Dennis can't move.

Luke's alarm brings an authority to his voice that erupts from his very gut. "Larry, you're gonna kill him! Stop!"

Like a wounded animal, Dennis stands against the wall howling in agony. The agony of cowardice.

Luke grabs fistfuls of sand with his free hand and tries to throw it at Larry, but it lands impotently at his feet.

And then, from nowhere but pure conjecture, from a notion not entirely empty of experience, Luke shouts, "You fuckin' moron! You fuckin' moron! Stop that!"

And Larry stops. In midpunch, he stops dead and turns to Luke, fear leaping in his eyes.

"Fuckin' moron." Luke bites out the magic words, but lower and more menacing now.

Wordlessly, Larry gets up and walks out of the sewer. Dennis, in tears, goes to help his brother.

"He's crazy, your friend. You know that, don't you?" Luke says.

Dennis doesn't answer. He helps Benny up and they make their way out of the sewer like wounded soldiers after a battle, leaning on one another. One bowed by pain, the other by shame.

"You better tell your parents what happened or he's gonna kill you one day," Luke shouts at their backs. "He's a lunatic! If anything happens to me, the police are going to come after you. Please, tell your parents! Please—please …"

But they're so deep in their own tragedy that they don't even turn to look at Luke.

And then they're gone. Luke is alone again. Tears begin to fill his eyes and run down the sides of his cheeks. He doesn't try to stop them. He tries to think of better days, but he can't—not family, not friends. Surely not his best friend, not Hank.

So he does the only thing he seems to be able to do. He weeps.

# CHAPTER EIGHTEEN

Larry's house, like much of Shorelane, is 1930s clapboard with a wooden front porch. Somewhere along the line someone talked the whole street out of its charm and into aluminum siding. Though less kindly looked after than many others, the O'Neill house is neat enough, lacking only the extra touch of flowers and interest.

It's less than ten minutes from the beach, but Larry drags his feet, taking almost twenty minutes to get home. Despite his stalling, his fat cheeks are still blotchy red, his ears crimson. Dirt stains his clothes, and his T-shirt is ripped where Benny tried to fight him off.

The front door is open, but Larry cuts around to the back door. He doesn't notice his father, crouched, working on an air conditioner that extends from a ground floor window.

But his dad sees him. Mr. O'Neill stands, and Larry immediately stops and backtracks. But not fast enough.

"Look at you, you fuckin' moron," Mr. O'Neill says, cuffing the boy upside his head. "What the hell have you been doing?"

Turning his head to shout in the open window, he calls to his wife in the same angry tones, "What the hell has he been doing? Goddamn it, Carol, can't you fuckin' keep your son clean?"

Carol never answers.

"So, moron, why don't you tell me what happened?"

Larry opens his mouth to speak, but before he can his dad gives him a knee in his stomach that sends him reeling backward.

"Forget it! Get upstairs and outta my sight." He throws down the wrench he's holding. "I can't fuckin' work around here!"

John O'Neill gets in his car and drives off, leaving all the tools and parts still sitting on the ground.

A fortyish-looking woman timidly peeks out the front door and watches the car drive off. Then she closes the door and the house is silent.

\* \* \*

Larry goes to his bedroom and closes the door. He knows his mother is in the hallway, but she purposely stands on the other side of the stairs so that she can't be seen.

He wishes she would take him in her arms the way she used to when he was little and his father got crazy. But she doesn't do that anymore. He thinks he's too big and ugly and she doesn't want to touch him, or maybe she's just scared and doesn't want his father to think she's on Larry's side. It's just like when his father gets crazy with his mother. Larry hides.

Sometimes he dreams of rushing in and helping her. Beating the shit out of his old man, making him run away and leave them alone. That would be good, just him and his mother.

Larry goes to his closet. He crawls under the hanging clothes and pulls out the new Monopoly game he got as a present from the guy next door, Ryan Michaels, for his eleventh birthday. It's still unopened. He likes the game, but you can't play Monopoly by yourself. And if you play with someone else, you might lose.

Under the game are some old sneakers, and under that, a wooden cigar box tied with string and rubber bands. Larry picks up the box, unties the strings, slips off the rubber bands and opens it. Inside is a small black gun. Just like the toy ones he had when he was little, only this one is real.

He stole it from his father's gun box almost two years ago and his dad still doesn't seem to know it's missing. He must have at least twenty more guns anyway. Some time later, Larry went back and took six bullets. He put them in the gun.

Lots of times he thinks about shooting his father. But what if he missed?

Maybe he'll bring the gun to the rain sewer. Yeah. Make that bum think twice about calling him a fuckin' moron. When you got a gun, nobody calls you nothin' but *yes, sir*. And it doesn't matter if you're only twelve. With a gun, he could be as big as his father.

Bigger.

# CHAPTER NINETEEN

Sixteen-year-old Ryan Michaels hears the shouting next door. As always, it makes him uncomfortable, but he's used to John O'Neill's temper. Ryan and his family have been listening to their neighbor's verbal abuse of his wife and son for years. The Michaels family prefers to think O'Neill limits himself to shouting and name calling, not physical abuse. If it were physical, they would have to call the authorities, and they sure as hell don't want to get involved with a nut like that. They've heard he has guns. Still, Ryan thinks he's heard things, things that sounded like a person falling down or hitting a wall. But he knew instinctively that his parents didn't want to hear about it, so he didn't say anything. He might have felt differently if the kid, Larry, were somebody he liked, but Larry is fat and sloppy and sweaty looking all the time. And he hears he's a bully, which explains why he's always hanging out with littler kids.

Thinking of Larry is unpleasant, so he does it as little as possible. It has to be lousy for the kid at home and not much better at school. Ryan knows the kids in Larry's class give him a hard time. Another reason why he hangs around with younger ones. But he knows that all you have to do is let him in once and you'll never get rid of him. Ryan is sixteen. He doesn't need a twelve-year-old hanger-on.

So, Ryan just closes his front door and goes up to his room. The house is empty. He'll go online, find a good website, maybe jerk off.

Maybe not jerk off since he has a date in about four hours with Ashley Beckmann. He's taking her down to the beach, the part that's closed off for the sea wall construction. Nobody will be around.

Or maybe jerking off isn't a bad idea—the last time he was with her, they were making out on her back porch and it was looking real good, but then he came all over his pants. He has time. His mother won't be home until five.

It's a knock-out idea. Not like jerking off for no reason, which always makes him feel a little guilty. This will almost be medicinal. Beautiful, the teenager thinks, racing up to the second floor two steps at a time.

# CHAPTER TWENTY

Luke has slept for almost two hours. He didn't think at his age he could cry himself to sleep, but that's what happened.

And now it's late afternoon and no one has come. Not the kids, not anyone. While he slept, the day cleared. The sun's dancing sparkles on the water has dissipated the threat of rain. Luke's spirits are calm. He hasn't given up on the children, but now he turns his attention to waiting for a dog walker or a beach jogger to come and save him.

More time passes. The day begins to lose light. The evening is warm, warm enough to walk on the beach, but no one does.

Luke's eyes stay trained on what he can see of the bay, the waves lapping softly against the sand. He remembers a beach party back in Australia—three girls, five guys. He couldn't have been more than fifteen and for some reason that he can't remember, he didn't want to go. But thank God he did—it turned out to be the most exciting night of his life.

Not that anything really happened. But it was Luke's first glimpse of possibilities.

Like every young boy, he knew about sex from reading and movies and bullshitting with the guys, but here it was, the real thing, inches away. A female body in a bikini, shivering, letting him hold her close. He could see her breasts, resting high in cups of silky fabric. More of the same material, but not much more, formed a triangle over what Luke knew had to be soft, pink skin and pubic hair the golden blond of her ponytail.

Nothing happened, but the feel of that exquisite soft body against his bare chest was enough. For a while.

That while turned out to be blessedly short. By fall, he'd had his first real sexual experience with Marcia Ann Seligson, his overweight neighbor with straw-like reddish hair. At seventeen, she was two years older than Luke, and she'd had sex with almost every boy in her high school class. She sought him out. Luke knew she was ugly and fat and that her face was pocked with craters from exploding pimples. He knew all these things but the only thing he could see were the rosy pink lips of her beautiful open vagina as it swallowed up his penis.

He spent the next two months shamelessly waiting on her doorstep every afternoon after school. He forsook everything— his friends, his sports, the other truly beautiful girls who came looking for him. It was only Marcia. And then an adorable cheerleader named Denise let him have sex with her. Suddenly Marcia didn't appeal to him anymore. She was still available, but she held no attraction. In fact, he wondered how she ever had. Luke was honing his sexual tastes.

Girls liked Luke for all the usual reasons they like good-looking boys. But there were other things. He was genuinely nice, mindful, and affectionate; he gave them all the attention that no one had ever bestowed on him. They say you play the same roles over and over again throughout your life, the ones you learned in childhood; abusive child makes an abusive parent. But sometimes there's an exception.

Luke liked the feel of a girl's small soft hand in his. He liked to caress their arms, run his hands down their backs, kiss them sweetly for no reason, and brush their hair back when a strand fell in their faces. He held doors open and guided them across streets with his hand on the small of their backs, looking down at them with obvious affection.

* * *

The buzz of a horsefly circling his head cuts into the sweet memories, propelling Luke back to his miserable present in a crappy town on Long Island, trapped in a rain sewer.

Maybe this is all there is. It's not as if he's robbing the world of a great talent. Where was he really going, anyway?

Like his mother always said: nowhere.

Hours have passed and not one person has walked by. The tunnel is filled with creaking sounds as trains steam past, shaking other beams that threaten to fall from the ceiling. An occasional piece of cement does drop but always on the other side of the tunnel.

There's enough daylight for Luke to see a chunk of loose cement right above him jiggle each time the beam shakes. It is only a small piece, not four inches square, but it's directly over his face. Luke tries to stop thinking about it, but it's hard.

The rats help.

They come as the last light of twilight fades, in the moments before full night. First, one slips silently out of the darkness. Luke catches the movement out of the corner of his eye. There's enough light left for him to see the furry, brownish-red creature tentatively making its way toward him. Luke shouts, and it darts away only to return seconds later followed by another, fatter one, whose belly almost touches the ground as it walks.

Luke scoops up a handful of sand and throws it in their direction. They scatter.

And then return, sooner than before. "Help! Help!" he screams.

The rats stop, but don't retreat. Two more slither out from the darkness. And then another comes from behind his head ...

# CHAPTER TWENTY-ONE

By five o'clock, Ryan Michaels has showered and swathed his armpits with enough deodorant to clog every sweat gland in his body. In case any droplet should miraculously seep through, the powerful aroma of Very Valentino would lay it low. In new Billabong jeans and a T-shirt, his hair spiked with gel, he's ready for action.

Action. Just what he expects. The last time he was with Ashley—five days and nearly twenty jerk offs ago—she let him put his hand inside her thong. He'd noticed that she had been finding excuses to stand close to him at the mall, brush against his arm, or accidentally touch him, all week.

She was ready.

Tonight it will happen.

He's sure.

He and Haskins, his best friend and one of the few other nonvirgins he knows, have been talking nonstop about how to handle every possible contingency. Ryan's nightmare is that she'll be wearing some kind of one-piece outfit, but Haskins said she would never wear anything so unsexy. Probably she'll have on a tight shirt that leaves her midriff exposed and a short skirt, or maybe a dress you could just slip up.

Ryan is conflicted. Should he try to get her into the back seat or do it in the front seat? If he suggests the back seat, she'll know what he has in mind. No, he told Haskins, the back seat is too in-your-face.

Haskins went nuts at that expression, laughing so hard he nearly fell off the bed.

The more they talked, the more impossible it seemed to Ryan. He decides he isn't even going to try. Unless she starts first.

* * *

At five minutes to six, Ryan is out the door and into his father's Dodge Stratus. At two minutes to six, he pulls up in front of Ashley's house and rings the doorbell at six p.m. on the dot.

Ashley opens it almost immediately, as if she's been waiting on the other side. To his immense relief, she's wearing a tight blouse that buttons down the front and shorts. She doesn't waste any time inviting him in, just grabs her purse, shouts, "See you later!" to no one he can see, and closes the door.

Ryan doesn't hear anyone answer.

It gets dark at about nine thirty. They have three hours to kill before they can park down at the beach.

# CHAPTER TWENTY-TWO

The day after the beach fiasco, Daisy half expects to see Luke. More than half. Surely if he were still in town he would stop down at the store to apologize or something? He liked her, she knows that. And she feels the same. What happened wasn't his fault. In fact, he acted heroically, throwing himself in front of her to ward off the stones. She would like to tell him that she didn't run off because she was angry. She was just upset about the children seeing them.

Daisy watches the front doors of Smilers all day. She has to be reprimanded twice, once to help a customer and once to pick up a comb that had slipped off her counter. When she isn't concentrating on the doors, she's daydreaming about her movie-star lover. It's the same scene over and over again. He appears at the door; she sees him through the glass but pretends she doesn't. He's dressed in a black silk shirt with black cord pants. He looks so gorgeous that everyone turns as he makes his way *directly* to her counter.

Over and over again in the daydream. He never gets there, but just seeing him move toward her makes her heart leap.

*God*, Daisy thinks, *am I in love? It's not possible. I barely know him.*

With that, the old uncertainties that always seem to haunt Daisy's decisions come flooding back. *It's not the way it's supposed to be*, she tells herself. All her life she's always believed, like millions of other young women, that you fall in love with someone because of his qualities: his kindness, character, intelligence, understanding, honor—the important things. Only then can you allow the enormous longing and passion to overshadow everything else in your life, to do what it's doing right now to Daisy.

Oh God, she knows this is wrong, but she has a strong life force and she knows how to give in when something is unstoppable.

With that understanding, she abandons all reasonable resistance and succumbs to the first real love of her life.

\* \* \*

Daisy, now a woman given fully to love, waits all day, but Luke doesn't come. Sometime late that afternoon, she decides to take a walk down to the beach. In her story, the one she's writing in her mind, she and Luke both go down to the beach at sunset, meeting up accidentally-on-purpose at the very spot of their picnic.

But around five, her friend, Mary Elizabeth, asks if she could stay late to do inventory. Mary Elizabeth's littlest daughter, Annie, is running a fever and she feels uncomfortable leaving her with the babysitter. Could Daisy help?

There's no way Daisy can say, "No, I want to walk down on the beach to look for this guy I'm in love with as of yesterday, blah, blah, blah" … Of course, she says yes. And that's the end of the beach; inventory goes on till eleven and there will be no romantic scene on the beach that late. Luke will be gone. Along with the possibility of Daisy ever getting out of Shorelane with him at her side.

That was probably her last chance to see him, she thinks. This man she loves so desperately will soon be a memory.

\* \* \*

To Daisy's surprise, inventory goes flawlessly, and she finishes before nine thirty. It's still light, barely, but say what you might about Shorelane, it's generally a safe community. You could walk on the beach without concern even after dark.

Daisy doesn't bother stopping in the ladies room to fix her makeup or comb her hair. She just grabs her purse and runs out the door.

"Hot date?" calls the manager as she speeds by. Daisy smiles but doesn't answer.

# CHAPTER TWENTY-THREE

The parking lot behind the beach is deserted. With the beach closed for repairs, there are no family barbecues or late-night parties. The cul-de-sac at the end of Longston Road is the "real" lovers' rendezvous in Shorelane, but just in case it doesn't work out, Ryan doesn't want to chance meeting anyone he knows. Instead, he chooses the deserted beach parking lot.

Neither Ryan nor Ashley spoke during the five-minute drive from the mall where they'd frittered away three hours pretending they weren't waiting for darkness. Now that it's almost upon them, the awkwardness has grown intense. Had either one been given the choice, they would have backed out. But no one has the courage to take that step.

Ryan surveys the parking lot and decides that parking right in the middle would put them farthest from the streetlights on either side. It's a warm night but not uncomfortably hot.

"It's nice out. Should I turn off the AC?" Ryan asks, zapping down his window.

"Sure, turn it off. It's great out." Ashley opens her window too. "I love the smell of the beach, don't you?"

"As long as it's not low tide." Ryan tries to smoothly ease his body from behind the steering wheel.

"Right," Ashley says, staring straight ahead as if she doesn't notice that he moved closer to her.

Good sign. She doesn't move away. Ryan thinks about asking her if she ever went clamming but that would require too long an answer.

One-word answers would allow him to make his moves without seeming impolite or like he isn't listening to her.

"Great moon, huh?" It isn't easy to free his left shoulder in so small a space. He needs to face her. Maybe he should take the chance of suggesting the back seat.

"Cool," she agrees, still not moving.

Ryan makes one big wrench and pulls his body around to face Ashley. Their legs are touching. If she moves away from him now, he'll think of another plan.

She doesn't.

This is it. Ryan puts his arms around Ashley and bends to kiss her. She responds the way he dreamed, even opening her mouth for his tongue. He feels his hard-on pressing against her thigh.

Some response button somewhere is pushed and at the same moment they both accelerate into high gear, unbuttoning, unzipping, pulling off shirts, sliding down pants, and kicking off shoes. In moments, they're both naked enough for sex.

The faint light from the streetlamps illuminates the scrambling and bouncing action in the car, allowing anyone approaching the one car in the parking lot to know exactly what is happening.

Anyone, like Daisy.

She's out of breath from rushing to beat the darkness. And as she arrives on the other side of the parking lot, her heart sinks. With what's happening inside the car, there's no way she can approach the beach entrance. She would have to walk right past the car. Not like it's daytime with people around, she's the only one. They would see her.

Daisy hangs back and watches as the last of twilight fades. She's a stupid girl. A stupid shop girl. Even thinking that Luke would be here … She was just a quick fuck, like those kids in the car. He probably doesn't even remember her name.

"Fuck him!" The words come out in a whisper as the foolish shop girl turns and leaves the parking lot.

# CHAPTER TWENTY-FOUR

The rats advance, sniffing the ground, moving aimlessly as if they have no interest in Luke. As if they don't even know he's there. Yet they keep moving in his direction. The one behind his head is the closest. He can almost feel it touching his hair.

Luke shakes his head violently, and it jumps back. But only for an instant. With his free hand, he scrambles around, searching for something to defend himself. He feels a slab of broken cement half wedged under his back. Grabbing the edge, he pries it back and forth until he's able to wrench it free.

The rat behind his head moves to the side of Luke's face, its pointed snout inches from Luke's mouth. Involuntarily, Luke jerks his head back; the rat rises up on his hind legs, half turns, then drops back on all fours in the same spot.

Luke keeps his hand still but moves his head back and forth forcefully enough to keep the rat away from his face. Shaking his head, he's able to herd him down past his shoulders, giving his hand room to lift the cement. He can feel the hairs of the animal graze his naked arm. Slowly, evenly, Luke raises his hand. The rat, emboldened by his superior position, barely moves out of the way.

Now Luke's arm is fully raised. He hesitates for just a moment then crashes the heavy chunk down on the rodent, catching him fully under the cement. Raising his arm up again, Luke smashes down on the writhing animal a second time. Wet globs of blood spray up in the air and drip down onto Luke's chest and face, but he keeps smashing until the thing is a smear of bloody pulp.

All the while, Luke screams. And screams.

# CHAPTER TWENTY-FIVE

Ryan cries out as the powerful orgasm shakes him. His cry seems to echo around them, on and on, filling the car. Slowly, Ryan realizes it isn't his voice. It's a bloodcurdling scream coming from outside, from the beach. A sound that could be made only by an ax-wielding madman charging at them.

Panicked, Ashley leaps up, slamming her arms against Ryan's head with such force that he falls back against the steering wheel, accidentally blasting the horn. Pain crunches into Ryan's kidneys. Wincing, he wrenches Ashley away and shoves her across the seat. In almost the same movement, he reaches for the ignition key, jams it in, and floors the gas pedal. The Dodge Stratus bucks over the parking lot, picking up speed as it heads toward the gate, neatly slicing off half a ball-cut boxwood bush as it shoots through the entrance and out into safety.

Both teenagers will be traumatized forever—or at least for the rest of the summer. Ryan does wonder briefly if the screams hadn't been for help, if he should have gone to help whoever was screaming. But he dismisses that notion. It isn't nearly as good as the scenario where he's the hero saving Ashley from the raving monster.

And the next day, when the police find the clothes floating in the sound, he thinks maybe it's from the victim and they're lucky to be alive. Ashley says it was because of his fast thinking. Ryan leaves it at that.

# CHAPTER TWENTY-SIX

In the sewer, Luke hears the horn and the screech of tires. He explodes in fury.

*Won't anybody help me!*

But he has helped himself. The killing of the rat serves as a warning to the others; they disappear back into the darkness. Not forever, Luke knows, but maybe for as long as the scent of their compatriot's blood is still fresh in their noses.

Shorelane, he thinks, will be the death of me. Isn't that the expression? This ordinary town that wasn't in any way interesting or special, this town he toyed with from the moment he first walked down Main Street. Unless some miracle takes place, this would be where he would die.

Suddenly it amuses him. The irony of it. That's good. Stay above it.

Luke allows himself the memory of how easy he thought this dumb little town was going to be. As usual, he had it all figured out, the challenge of it: wits against adversity. Like a movie where the hero is deposited in a strange town with no money or friends and has to find both and get laid in forty-eight hours. Great stuff for a romantic comedy. Maybe he'll write a treatment. Yeah, right.

Still, Luke thinks, he could start again. No shortcuts this time. If only he could have the chance.

The moon's reflection is bright on the water; the night seems especially light. It must be clear. No clouds. But Luke smells impending rain, that soft, wet, clean smell.

Surprisingly, he doesn't feel frightened. Even after the rats. Instead, he's almost relaxed. Is this his mind's preparation for death? It could be, Luke thinks. After all, people don't go screaming into death; instead they seem to slip gently into it.

His mother always accused him of not thinking ahead, but maybe that was the best thing he ever didn't do. When you can't fight the inevitable, just slide into it. What the hell. Like she said, he was going nowhere anyway.

Exhaustion and the heavy scent of the coming rain slide Luke down into the comfort of sleep. At the brink of the thick, warm abyss … he jerks awake.

*No! Goddamn it!*

*No fucking way!*

*I'm not going to die!*

# CHAPTER TWENTY-SEVEN

SUNDAY, JULY 3

It's early, before nine in the morning, when the children arrive at the beach. The day is summer warm and bright, and the water sparkles, glistening in the sunlight. From the shore, they can see what looks like two dots riding the waves in the bay. Curious, they follow them down to the water's edge.

The dots come closer, clarifying themselves into Coast Guard speedboats. On each boat they can make out men standing on the stern dragging long poles in the water.

"They lookin' for sharks?" Benny asks.

"Ya think?" Dennis looks to Larry.

"They got sharks here," Larry answers. With the gun in his pocket, he's feeling like a boss, a real big shot. It doesn't even bulge in his oversized pants.

"I saw one like last week," he tells his crew. "Not the whole thing, just the fin sticking up."

"No shit!" The twins are always ready for a Larry story, no matter how implausible.

"Maybe it was a porpoise," Charley says. "They got them here, too, ya know."

"What are you, some kind of asshole? Don't you think I can tell the difference between a porpoise and a shark?"

As usual, Charley backs down stammering that he didn't mean that, just that he read there were going to be a lot of porpoises in the bay this summer. Something about new mating grounds. He could see from Larry's face how wrong he was.

"Could you tell how big the shark was?" Charley tries covering.

"About forty feet or so. Something like that."

Lucy rolls her eyes, and makes a quiet "yeah, right" sound.

Larry looks at the little girl. Paying no attention to her isn't good enough. She's always doing something that annoys him, and the worst part is that she doesn't give a shit. He can't figure her out. Why isn't she afraid of him? Charley and the twins are much bigger and they're scared shitless. He hates Lucy. If he shoots the homeless guy, which he's probably going to do, he would have to kill Lucy too. Nobody else would tell on him, but he couldn't count on her. Yeah, he would shoot her. But just to make sure, he would do it when no one was watching.

That decided, Larry goes on to describe how the head of the shark was so far from the fin he thought it was another fish.

"Maybe it was." Stupid Dennis, trying to get in on the story.

"No, jerkhead," Larry says, rapping him on the side of his head hard enough to throw him off balance.

"I only meant it coulda been a herd of them." Still trying.

"School, asshole." Charley jumps onto the winning team.

"On Sunday?" Dennis can't let go.

With the exception of Dennis, they all fall down in hysterics. Even Lucy plops herself down on the sand, laughing.

Finally, their attention moves to the speedboats coming into the dock at the far end of the beach. This looks like action. With the little girl bringing up the rear, all five children run down the shore toward the boats. It's a good quarter mile; by the time they get there, the boats have docked.

"Was it a shark?" Larry calls to the Coast Guard officers, squinting against the morning sun.

"Hey, son." The officer looks down at him doubtfully. "You kids aren't supposed to be on the beach. Better get outta here now."

"Okay," Larry says, "but was it a shark?"

It feels good to be talking to a cop when you have a gun in your pocket. Like they're equals, except the cop doesn't know it. But if he gives Larry a hard time, he'll find out soon enough. Larry could take out the gun and shoot him before anyone could do anything. He's close enough not to miss.

But he isn't going to do that. He's going to save the gun for Luke. And Lucy. For sure Lucy.

"It wasn't a shark," the officer says. "It wasn't anything."

But the officer standing alongside interjects, "Tell 'em, Frank. Maybe it'll teach 'em not to play down here alone."

"You're right," Frank says. Getting down on one knee, he speaks gently to the children. "Looks like somebody maybe drowned here."

The children are shocked.

"Who was it?" Charley asks.

"We don't know yet."

"You see," the other cop gives his safety lesson, "that's what happens when you go swimming and nobody's around. If you get in trouble, nobody can help you."

"Did you find him? Can we see him?" Larry starts climbing the side of the pier.

"Hey, stay down, kid. There's nothing to see. We didn't find the body."

"So how do you know somebody drowned?" Benny asks.

"We found his jacket and shoes." The officer reaches into a wooden crate and holds up Luke's dripping wet jacket and shoes.

As if on cue, all five children move in toward each other. They never take their eyes off the clothes the cop is holding up.

"Did you see anyone around wearing this jacket?"

The children huddle even closer together, a knot of small bodies.

"Did you?" The officer asks again.

They shake their heads firmly.

"You're sure?"

They continue to shake their heads.

"You're not sure?"

Now they nod furiously.

"Good." He stands up. "Now beat it and don't come down here alone, or I'll have to tell your parents. Got that?"

More nodding as the children back up and speed down the beach, even Lucy running fast enough to almost catch up.

# CHAPTER TWENTY-EIGHT

Word of the drowning spreads quickly through Shorelane. They were talking about it in Smilers Cool Shoppe all morning, but Daisy has an unexpected toothache that requires a dentist appointment. She decides since she isn't going to get paid for the morning, she'll go in after lunch, and she goes directly to the coffee shop to meet Mary Elizabeth. It's noon before she hears the news.

"They think maybe it was suicide because they found his jacket and shoes washed up in the same place near the pier. Like he left them there and then drowned himself," Mary Elizabeth says.

"Oh my god, how awful. Who was it?"

"They don't know. So far nobody's missing. I mean, nobody who lives here anyway."

Daisy almost stops breathing. A shiver travels down the nerves in her stomach and spikes out into her inner thighs.

Mary Elizabeth sees her intense reaction. "What?"

Instinctively, Daisy moves her hand to her cheek. "Oh—I— my tooth …"

"God, I thought it was about the guy who drowned."

Somehow, Daisy manages to smile. She stands up, leans over, and picks her purse up from the floor.

"Aren't you going to eat?" Mary Elizabeth asks.

"I can't. My mouth is still numb. See you back at the store." She throws her friend a purposely crooked smile and leaves without waiting for a reply.

Once outside, she walks quickly toward the bottom of Main Street, crosses the wide plaza, and climbs the circular marble steps to the police station. The entrance room, with its rows of wooden benches, is empty except for one policewoman manning the front desk.

The policewoman doesn't look up when Daisy walks in. She continues to not look up while Daisy stands uncomfortably in front of her desk. Her usual dealings with criminals or families of criminals, she feels, gave her license for rude behavior. Taking her sweet time, she examines a sheaf of papers then slowly lifts her head to look at Daisy.

"Yes?" Along with an unspoken, *And why are you disturbing my important work?*

"Hello," Daisy smiles, her normal greeting for strangers, and is met with open annoyance. Haltingly, she begins, "The man who drowned …"

The policewoman offers no help.

Daisy continues. "Could you tell me about him?"

No answer.

"I … I think I might have known him or something."

"There is no man. We don't have a body."

"But I thought …"

"We have some clothes. You wanna see the clothes?"

LITTLE CREW OF BUTCHERS

"I don't know. Maybe I was wrong …" Daisy begins to form a "thank you," but the woman has already pushed the intercom button. There is no answer.

"Just wait here," she says and disappears through a doorway. Daisy would have fled, but she's in the habit of taking orders—especially from authority figures. So she waits. A few moments later, the door opens again, and a policeman Daisy recognizes as Helmut Smite beckons her into a long corridor.

"How are you, Daisy?" he asks.

"Okay, thanks."

The policeman opens a door to the closet of an office. "You wanna sit over there?" Helmut asks, pointing to a wooden folding chair squeezed against the desk in his tiny cubicle.

Daisy sits.

"Kathy tells me you were asking about the drowned man. Do you think you know him?"

"I don't know."

"Tell me about it. Is it some guy you met here in town?"

Just from the leer on his face, Daisy knows Helmut is going to want to know all about everything. And everything is just what Daisy doesn't want to tell him.

In the beginning it is always easier to push Daisy than it is to push anyone else. Indeed, it's so effortless that the pusher could be fooled into thinking he could go on and on. But at a certain point, Daisy stops and nothing, not even good reasons, can make her move.

Helmut, with his steady leer, is getting close to that point.

"The policewoman outside said there were clothes. Could I see the clothes?" Daisy asks.

"A boyfriend maybe?" Helmut isn't ready to pass up a good fuck story.

"No," says Daisy. "My boyfriend's in the hospital. He just had surgery for hemorrhoids." She watches with a certain pleasure as the delicious expectation in Helmut's face collapses. Daisy's sense of humor isn't always noticeable, but it's there.

"Yeah, right," he says, diving reluctantly back into the boredom of Shorelane police work. He reaches into a cardboard box next to his desk.

While Helmut is bending down, Daisy resolves that no matter what he shows her, she won't react. She barely waits for him to lift the two large clear plastic bags and drop Luke's jacket and shoes on the desk before she blurts, "No one I know," and shoots to her feet, halfway out the door before Helmut can blink.

"Sorry, Helmut, can't help you."

And she's gone.

Helmut looks up in time to catch only the last of the disappearing act. No hot story there anyway, he thinks.

# CHAPTER TWENTY-NINE

The air in front of Daisy swims with tiny flashes of light. It feels so hot and thick—the weight of it seems to pound against her head as she fights her way down the corridor to the entrance and out the front door. Fortunately, no one is blocking her pathway. She wouldn't have seen them.

Bursting out into the bright sun, dripping with perspiration, dizzy from shock and pain, Daisy trips down the steps, searching frantically for a place, any place—a bench, a plot of grass—anywhere to throw herself down just to catch her breath.

What if it was her fault? Not suicide, but maybe he was hurt worse than she thought. One of the rocks did hit him. Daisy remembers the blood on Luke's forehead and her stomach turns. But it was nothing; he seemed fine. He said he was fine! But what if he had a concussion and got dizzy later and fell and the tide came in ...

Daisy finds a patch of grass behind a row of rhododendrons and sits down hard on the ground.

That's when she begins to cry.

She feels a terrible loss. All the expectations, all the possibilities, no matter how foolish, had existed, even if only in her dreams. Now she can't even have them there. Gone. Irreparably destroyed. Luke would never be in her life again. In any life. He was gone. Poor Luke.

Maybe it had been stupid to fall in love with a stranger, but Daisy had. And she should have had the courage to act on it. So what if it wasn't the right thing? Fuck the right thing! People hardly ever did the right thing anyway, Daisy included. Most of the time, in fact, she did nothing. As if that were safe. But just like omission could be a lie, doing nothing could allow wrong to be done.

Daisy fell in love with Luke and now he's dead and she's partly to blame. Maybe not "to blame" exactly, but suppose she'd stayed? She might have saved him. If only she wasn't so goddamn modest or embarrassed … or cowardly.

It's past lunch now. The plaza is empty. Still, Daisy stays out of sight behind the bushes. She keeps crying. She feels like she could cry all day and still not cry out her sadness.

But finally the tears stop. There are things to do. Things to do for Luke.

Should she call the papers? No, they would want to know too much, but she has to tell someone. Maybe his friend, Gwyneth Paltrow, or Gwyneth's mother, Blythe Danner. It would be easier to call Blythe because she was sort of a New York actress and would probably be more accessible than a Hollywood star.

But would she be listed in the phone book or on the internet? Daisy frowns. Probably not. Still, she must belong to the actor's union. Daisy read about them maybe going on strike a few months earlier, and then it was settled but she remembers it was some organization called Equity. She could call Equity and if she tells them how important it was and how it was about a friend drowning, they might give her Blythe Danner's phone number.

Daisy decides to miss work in the afternoon as well. She'll call the manager and say her tooth is still too swollen to come in. She stands, smooths her wrinkled cotton skirt, checks to see that no one she knows is around, and comes out from behind the bushes and hurries up Main Street in the direction of her house.

As she crosses behind the stores at the top of the hill, she thinks she catches a glimpse of the kids—Lucy's friends—way down at the end of the street in the little playground near the day camp. But when she looks back, they're gone.

She doesn't want to see them anyway. What had started out as merely embarrassing has turned tragic. Eventually the police will get around to her and the kids. She will see them soon enough.

* * *

Daisy gets lucky. Mrs. McDonnell isn't in her usual rocker on the porch, so Daisy doesn't have to come up with a story to explain her swollen eyes and red nose.

She runs right up to her room where she left her cell phone on the charger. First thing she tries is information for New York, but there's no listing for Blythe Danner. Then she gets the phone number for Actor's Equity and dials it.

"I'm trying to get in touch with Blythe Danner. It's very important, and I don't have her phone number," she tells the young man who answers the phone.

He's probably a struggling actor with a deep personal knowledge of rejection, and even though there's no way he can give out anyone's phone number, he's kind to Daisy.

"I'm sorry, we're not allowed to give out numbers, but if you want I can give you her agent and he can help you get in touch with her." Daisy takes the agent's name and number and thanks the young man. He tells her good luck, and it makes her feel a little better.

She dials the agent and an assistant answers. From her voice, the agent's assistant is a middle-aged woman not long on patience. She turns Daisy down flat.

"You don't understand," Daisy says. "There's been a tragedy. Something terrible has happened to a friend of hers. It's someone her daughter was just in a film with, but she's friendly with him, too. In fact, they're close friends."

Now the assistant is interested. "Who is it?"

"I think I should wait and tell her."

"What movie was it?"

"I'm not sure, but I think it was *Walking Wonders*."

"*Walking Wonders*?"

"Yes, it just wrapped. I haven't seen it yet."

"I never heard of it. What's the guy's name?"

"I'm sorry, but I don't think I should …"

"Forget it, then. Unless I know who it is, I'm not giving out any numbers."

"But I have to be the one to talk to her. This is going to be very painful, and he was a good friend of mine too. I was sort of there, so I can really explain it."

"Look. You have to tell me who we're talking about."

Unsure whether she should give out his name, she hesitates. Then blurts out, "Lucas Baird."

"Who?"

A small itch of discomfort touches Daisy. "Lucas Baird?" she says with the hint of a question.

"Never heard of him. What is he, an extra?"

Daisy's voice grows timid. "Actually, I think ... at least I thought he was sort of one of the leads."

"No way, honey. We know pretty much everything that Gwyneth does, and I can tell you she was never in anything called *Wonders*, or whatever. And for sure not with anyone named Lucas Baird. Someone's pulling your leg."

"Thank you," Daisy says, and clicks off the phone.

She sits quietly for a few moments. Long enough to give herself time to rationalize, find some possibility that would allow her to believe even part of Luke's story. Foolish as it seems, she just isn't ready to stop.

But who could she ask? No point in looking in the newspapers. If Luke truly is a movie actor and the film with Gwyneth does exist, Daisy would be able to find it on the Internet. She has a laptop, but Mrs. McDonnell doesn't have wireless; she'd have to go to Starbucks.

Daisy doesn't bother combing her hair or trying to hide the tear stains on her face. She walks slowly down the stairs and out of her house, an unhappy combination of dread, disappointment, and deep sadness weighing on her heart.

# CHAPTER THIRTY

Larry spots Daisy coming up Main Street and rushes the other kids out of the playground. The conversation with the police has left them too frightened to notice anything wrong.

"What are we gonna do?" Dennis asks.

"Nothing, stupid," Larry says, punching Dennis's shoulder. "He's dead—didn't you hear the cops? He drowned."

"Yeah, he's drowned," Benny says, easily abandoning his twin.

"What if the cops ask us about him?" Charley says.

"I don't know nothin', do you?" Larry says.

Immediately, the twins shrug and shake their heads, mumbling no, not me, not me. After an instant, Charley joins in.

They all turn to look at Lucy. She stares right back at them.

That's when Larry knows for sure that he's going to have to shoot her. If his father ever finds out what they did to the guy in the sewer, even though he was a homeless and he wouldn't have even cared ... Most of the time he whacked Larry around without any reason, but when he figured out he had one ...

No way Larry is going to take that chance. Anyway, it wouldn't be that hard to shoot Lucy. She's just a little kid; she can't really fight back. All he'd have to do is get her someplace alone and put a bullet in her head. He wouldn't take a chance on shooting her in the heart because you never know exactly where the heart is. It's supposed to be on the left side, but sometimes in a movie somebody would get shot in the middle of the chest and they said it was in the heart. He wouldn't take any chances, he'd blow her brains out. And he wouldn't have to worry about the gun. Nobody knows he has it. His father hasn't missed it in two years. And then, after, he'd find a place to bury it.

Larry puts his palm on the gun and rubs it lightly. It feels good to be armed. Like when police say in a movie, "Hey, watch it, the guy's armed!" He feels powerful, like nobody—not even adults—can push him around.

Charley is getting scared and making excuses for his sister. "She's just a kid—who's gonna listen to her? Besides, she's not gonna say anything anyway, right, Luce?"

Lucy shrugs her shoulders and bends down to pick up a stick. She pokes aimlessly at a hole in the dirt while the boys watch.

Charley is desperate. "When she does that with her shoulders that means yes," he says. Lucy doesn't disagree so they accept Charley's word and move on.

Larry almost smiles. He's never going to have to worry about that little pain in the ass again.

Then Charley has another thought. "What if that lady Daisy says something?"

"Yeah, right," Larry says. "Like she's gonna say she was fucking this guy on the beach with kids watching."

"I guess not." But Charley has another worry. "What if they find the sewer and some of our things are still there?"

No one can worry better than Charley, but this time he has a point.

"You took my mother's curtain rods," Lucy says to Larry. "And you didn't give them back."

"So? They're gonna know it's your mother's curtain rod? It's got her name on it?"

"The police got special things where they can find out where anything comes from," Charley says. "They always find out where the guy's suit was made or the dry cleaners, things like that."

And then Charley remembers that they took some of his father's tools. Those would be easy to trace. "We gotta go back and get my dad's stuff."

"Not me," says Benny.

Dennis nods his head in agreement.

"Chickenshit," says Charley. "You coming, Larry?"

Larry doesn't want to, but he can't look scared in front of the twins. And anyway, he isn't scared. The guy's dead, and it would be fun to make the twins go. They'd piss in their pants.

"Sure thing. Come on!" Larry points to the twins. "Everybody!"

# CHAPTER THIRTY-ONE

Daisy looks through two movie websites, something called IMDb. com and a Who's Who of Hollywood. No *Walking Wonders*, no Lucas Baird.

Oh boy, is she dumb.

And in love. Crying her eyes out for some goddamn hustler; some phony who—if he wasn't dead—would be laughing his head off about the little shopgirl he fucked in Shorelane.

But he *is* dead, and she's the one who can laugh. Except she can't. If she was smart and really worthwhile, she would laugh. She wouldn't feel so hurt. Hurt at being tricked by someone she so foolishly loved. And, stupidly or not, trusted.

A better woman would feel demeaned by such lies, Daisy thinks. She would feel outrage. But she doesn't. Instead, she feels ashamed of herself—for not being outraged.

# CHAPTER THIRTY-TWO

The small band of children trudge down the beach to collect their things from the sewer, careful to avoid being seen. Instead of going through the parking lot, they skirt it and go by way of the bushes lining the perimeter. They slip quickly through the broken fence and run over the weed-covered dune and down onto the beach.

The tide is low, and the exposed sand is covered with rocks, broken shells, and clumps of seaweed. Everywhere there is the pungent smell of fish and clams and black muck.

The construction site is empty, the workers still off enjoying the Fourth of July holiday. No cops are around either. They are all waiting down by the docks where the current would take a body.

Charley is ready first. He's nervous about the police finding his father's tools. "C'mon," he whispers, "let's go in and get the stuff before somebody sees us."

Just as he says it, a man walking his dog passes by on the road beyond the parking lot. The kids duck down and stay quiet; the man is far enough away that the protruding dunes easily hide them.

"You go, Charley," Larry says when they reach the sewer. "You know what your old man's stuff looks like."

"So do you. You took it." Charley is surprised at himself. He never gave orders to Larry before.

Lucy nods, agreeing with her brother and giving Larry and the twins a rare smile.

Larry can't afford to lose control so he says that everybody's going in and shoves the twins toward the sewer. But Benny won't move.

"What's your problem, asshole? The guy's drowned. His body's not even there! He's out in the bay somewhere."

"So you go first," Benny says, prodded either by an unusual burst of courage or terror.

Rather than risk anarchy, Larry goes toward the sewer. The others follow a good ten feet behind. Just at the entrance, Larry stops. Why is he scared? He has a gun. A strong feeling of power comes over him. Everything is different with a gun.

The twins and Charley hang back, but Lucy keeps walking. She passes Larry, and he lets her quietly disappear into the sewer opening. Barely ten seconds pass before she shoots out, horror widening her eyes and distorting her face.

"He's in there!" she screams. "And he's got blood all over him! He's dead!"

The four boys gasp in horror. Without saying a word, they spin on their heels and start scrambling up the dunes.

That's when they hear Luke's shouts. "Wait! I'm here! I'm here! Come back!"

* * *

The children stop dead in their tracks, barely breathing. Luke keeps shouting, but they don't answer. Not even Lucy, who is still in shock from the sight of Luke's face covered in the rat's blood and guts.

Luke pleads for them to answer.

Lucy, who was below the dune, pulls on Charley's foot. "Charley, he's hurt. I saw the blood."

"We're not going back there," Dennis says. "Suppose he's just pretending, just waiting for us to come back so he can kill us?"

"I'm not going!" says Benny.

Dennis nods.

Lucy looks at her brother, but he is not on her side.

"Maybe Dennis is right. Maybe he's just waiting for us. We're going home. C'mon!" Charley grabs her arm, pulling her up the dune.

But she won't budge. "He's bleeding. I saw."

Charley knows he can't leave his sister, but he's scared to death that Luke will come charging out and kill them all. Then he gets an idea.

"Look, Luce, we'll tell Mom and Dad; they'll get the police to take him to the hospital if he's hurt. That would be okay, right?"

"I guess. Yeah, that would be good," Lucy says. Freed of her terrible responsibility, she starts scrambling up the dune.

The others are halfway across the parking lot when Larry changes his mind.

"You take the shithead and get her out of here," he tells Charley. "We're going back."

The twins look at him aghast. It's their worst nightmare, but horrified as they are, they say okay, grimacing all the while.

"You got a problem with that?" the bully asks them.

"No! No way." In unison.

And trailing some feet behind their leader, the twins follow Larry back over the dunes to the sewer.

"You first," Larry points midway between them.

Naturally, both boys point to the other. Larry watches while they argue. He lets them come to blows, and only when Benny has Dennis near tears in an armlock, he points to Benny and says, "You, asshole."

To anyone else in the world, Benny would say, how come? Why me? But not to Larry. He slowly creeps into the sewer, ready to jump back at each step.

The darkness swallows the boy, and for a moment there is silence, and then he calls out in a loud brave voice, "Okay, guys, you can come in."

"See, I told ya." Big shot Larry waves Dennis in. "You're just chickenshit. C'mon."

# CHAPTER THIRTY-THREE

Luke is overjoyed to see somebody, anybody, but of all the any-bodies he'd choose it wouldn't be these three. Still, at least they didn't abandon him.

"Where are the others?" he asks.

"None of your business," Larry says.

"Look, kid," Luke ignores the hostility and tries to talk to Larry in the most unemotional, reasonable voice he can muster. "I don't know why you're angry. If I did something to you, I'm sorry. I just want to get out of here. Are you going to help me or not?"

"What'll ya give me?"

"I don't have anything to give you. I'm homeless, remember?"

"I want a hundred dollars. Maybe five hundred."

"Yeah!" The twins jump in. "Us too. We want the same."

"No way you're getting what I get," says Larry. "I decide how much. Got any problem with that?"

Of course they don't.

"I'll give you the money," Luke says. "I don't have five

hundred, but I have some. It's in my pocket. Get me out and you can have it all."

"Yeah, right. Like we're gonna fall for that. Why don't ya get it from your cousin Mel Gibson?"

"Get me out, and I'll get you all the money you ask for."

Silence. And that's when Luke loses it.

"For fuck's sake, just get me out! Do you hear me? You know what kind of pain I'm in? You gotta get me out!"

But Larry has lost interest. He's found one of the curtain rods from Charley's house, and he swings it hard toward Luke's head. Luke winces, but Larry stops the rod inches from Luke's face, raising it up until it touches the ceiling. He whacks it across the loose piece of cement.

"Hey, watch it!" Luke shouts, slapping his free hand up to protect his face. He can't reach far enough to shield his eyes. "That's loose! It's gonna fall on me."

"No kidding?" Larry says. He's found a new game. He pokes the cement ever so slowly and gently with the rod, carefully sliding the end under a loose corner and prying it up. Two small pieces break loose and fall.

The twins gasp. Luke yelps and twists his head as far to the side as he can, but one piece lands on his cheek, hitting hard enough to break the skin. A patch of blood wells up, dribbling back into Luke's hair.

"If that big piece falls, it could kill me. Do you understand? You could kill me."

"Everyone thinks you're dead anyway."

"What are you talking about?"

"They found your jacket and shoes in the bay. They think you drowned. You oughta be grateful. I'm saving your life."

"How's that?"

"I'm gonna knock that cement shit away from you." Larry smiles at his cohorts, who have to snap back from their own horror to appreciate his humor.

"Wanna help?"

Benny reluctantly takes the rod and taps once on the ceiling, safely away from the loose patch of cement.

"Here, jerkoff, not like that. You want it to fall on him?" Larry grabs the pole and slams it hard against the ceiling. Amazingly only dust falls, but the larger piece loosens, hanging at a forty-five degree angle from the ceiling. One more touch, one more train rumble, and it will certainly fall.

"Stop! Please!" Luke shouts, but Larry keeps slamming the rod against the cement. "What do you want from me?"

"Shut up. I told ya, I'm saving your fuckin' life."

"Please don't keep knocking. It's going to fall on me."

"I don't think so."

"Goddamn it, of course it will!"

"Wanna bet?"

Luke doesn't answer. He's been stupid. He's played into Larry's hands. The kid wants to kill him and he won't stop until he does. But he wants to do it with a lot of noise and Luke is helping.

That's it, he decides. He's not going to say another word. Luke braces himself, closing his eyes and keeping his head stretched as far out of the way as possible. The movement of his free arm is too limited for his hand to cover more than his ear. Not that it makes any difference. The cement is poised directly over his head and weighs at least four or five pounds. If it falls straight, the path of least resistance, from that height, it will kill him.

Summoning all the mental energy he has left, Luke tries to

stop caring, to shut down the survival instinct and just commit suicide. He's got every reason. Why is he fighting? Let him kill me, he thinks. One merciful blow and it will all be over. No more horrific struggles—not drowning, being eaten by rats, dying of thirst.

Now Luke prays for the cement to end his agony.

But as much as Larry pokes and pries, the slab stays at the same angle, its corner wedged tightly into a beam. After five minutes of fruitless effort, Larry tires of holding the rod up and lets it fall, crashing down just below Luke's throat.

Luke yells out in pain.

"I gotta take a piss," Dennis says. "Let's go."

"I got an idea," Larry says. "Do it here. Right on Loki."

The twins are so alarmed they start giggling.

"Let's all do it. C'mon." Larry starts to unzip his fly. The twins follow suit.

"I'm not getting close enough for him to grab my dick," Benny says.

"Hey, me neither," says his brother.

"You don't have to get that close, butthead," Larry says, taking his penis out of his pants. "All you do is hold it up like this and hold your finger on the end so that it shoots further. Like this." With that, he pees in a long, hard line that arcs up and comes down right in Luke's face. "Bull's-eye!"

The twins stand on either side of Larry spraying their urine all over Luke's head.

"Open your mouth, pisshead!" Larry shouts.

Luke lies stone still, expressionless, receiving the degradation with stoic dignity. This, the final humiliation, crushes him, replacing any trace of self-esteem with disgust.

The boys are screaming with laughter. "Yeah, pisshead!" Dennis shouts.

Benny is laughing so hard some of his urine spatters Larry's sneakers.

Without letting go of his penis, Larry uses his other hand to shove Benny off his feet. The boy falls hard against the rough wall of the sewer, scraping his side as he goes down.

"Fuckin' moron! I should make you lick it up," Larry shouts.

Benny starts crying, from the fall and the fear, and the game is ruined.

"Let's go," Larry says. Meekly, the twins follow him out of the sewer.

Luke hasn't moved.

# CHAPTER THIRTY-FOUR

All the way home, Lucy keeps asking Charley what they're going to do about the homeless man.

"We'll tell Mom and Dad, right? You said."

For a long time Charley won't answer her. Finally, out of nowhere, like he just thought it up himself, he says, "We'll tell Mom and Dad. We can say how we tried to get the stuff off him and we couldn't, but we thought we could for a couple of days and that's why we didn't tell them before. And then we can say how we brought him food and all."

"Are we going to tell about Larry and how he hit him?"

"No, stupid. We're not going to say anything about Larry or the twins."

"But what about how Larry was saying the man was our prisoner?"

"No way. You want Larry to pound your head like he did the homeless guy? Listen, you just shut up, and I'll say everything."

"Okay."

"Okay?" Charley is always surprised when Lucy agrees with him.

Lucy nods her head, yes, and then she wants to know how come Larry is always so mean and no one does anything about it. Charley says how come she doesn't notice that Larry is twice as big as everyone else and could beat the shit out of anyone who gives him trouble?

"So why don't we tell Daddy? Larry couldn't beat him up."

"Yeah, so is Daddy gonna go to school with us every day? And then stick around after and on the weekends and make sure nobody cuts your tongue out?"

Lucy gasps.

"Now what are you going to say?"

"Nothing."

"Good. Leave it to me. I'll tell them about the homeless guy, and they'll call the cops or whatever, and we never have to see him again."

* * *

Mrs. Adler is in the kitchen chopping carrots for vegetable soup when the children return. She hears them close the door and calls out, "Charley! Lucy! In here, in the kitchen."

With one last warning to keep quiet, Charley goes down the hallway, Lucy following.

The minute the children walk into the room they know their mother is annoyed.

"Where were you?" she directs her question at Charley.

"No place."

"I hope no place was not that construction site at the beach. Sergeant Dasto told me he saw a whole bunch of you down there."

"Not today," Charley said.

"It doesn't make any difference *when*. The point is, is that how you take care of your sister? Taking her to dangerous places? When I hear things like that, Charley, I feel like I'm making a mistake trusting you with important responsibilities. And frankly, I say to myself, maybe I should show you what a lack of responsibility means. Maybe you would understand it better if you had to miss the Fourth of July picnic. How about that?"

Before Charley can answer, Lucy speaks up.

"We were only going down there because the twins said a little kitten got lost from its mother and we should find it and bring it back … It was borned only three days ago and there was a big black dog looking for it and I made Charley take me because I thought if I could find it I could take care of it. Charley didn't want to go."

Charley looks with amazement at his sister. His sister who almost never cries has big blobs of tears running down her cheeks.

"But then when we got there …"

"Oh, honey." Leddy Adler melts at her little girl's tears. Drying her hands on her apron, she bends down and takes the sobbing child in her arms. "I'm so sorry."

In a much kinder, more understanding voice, she says to Charley, "I still don't want you to take any chances with her. I know it's a big responsibility for you. I'm sorry you have to do it, but it's only a little longer and then maybe I can stay home more. Okay, sweetie?"

And she reaches out to her son, who moves uncomfortably toward her.

When Lucy calms down, her mother says she could use their help putting the gardening tools back in the garage. Grateful for the opportunity to escape their lies, both children run to the backyard. While Leddy watches from the window, they gather up the tools and bags of pull weeds and drag them to the garage.

"That was good what you did for me, Luce. Thanks."

"Are we still going to tell them about the homeless man?"

"I don't think so. Then it would be like you lied."

"I did lie."

"Yeah, but then I'm in trouble again. And you too. They'll be so angry with the lie that we'll all get punished. Even worse than not going to the picnic. We gotta find another way to get him help."

"What about Daisy?"

"Hey, yeah. We could find her and tell her and she could get the ambulance. We could ask her not to tell that we told her."

"She's nice. She wouldn't tell. Can we go now?"

The children run back into the house. Lucy leaves it to Charley. He says something about wanting to go over to Smilers to get some pencils, but Leddy says no. It's Sunday; the stores close early. Besides, Dad will be home soon and maybe they'd do something special for the rest of the afternoon.

Lucy gets excited. "Could we go to the petting farm?"

There isn't a trace of Luke left in her mind. Though there are times when Lucy seems almost wise, she's only seven. Petting farms come before homeless strangers, no matter how desperate their situation is.

"I don't know. Let's wait to see what Daddy says."

"I'll put on my jeans just in case." Lucy runs upstairs to change. Leddy Adler sighs. She hates the petting farm. She always makes the children wear long pants and long-sleeved shirts, and she still cringes every time they hug one of the filthy baby animals. She washes every piece of their clothing when they get home and insists they scrub themselves, hair and all, immediately.

Charley, who at ten has a more developed sense of priorities—and has outgrown petting farms—assumes his natural worry stance. He thinks they should find Daisy while it's still afternoon. He hadn't seen Luke, but he knows a person could bleed to death.

"I don't want to go to the petting farm, Mom. Can I stay home?"

"Don't worry about it, honey. We'll find someplace else to go." That exhausts Charley's ideas for the moment. He'll wait until his father gets home and, in the meantime, think of some other excuse to get away.

He'll find Daisy and she'll get the ambulance and fix everything.

# CHAPTER THIRTY-FIVE

The lies Luke told keep spinning through Daisy's mind.

She's hurt, the same hurt someone in love would feel if they had been betrayed. On top of that, she still feels a longing for Luke. She misses him, and it shames her. She has to do something radical to wipe out the sick feelings of disgust.

It's a dazzling Sunday on the Fourth of July weekend. All of New York will have rushed out to the beaches on Long Island; if Daisy chooses, she can hop a train to New York and wander around a relatively empty city. No one will have any idea that she lives in ugly little Shorelane or works at a semi-drugstore; they wouldn't know she'd been deceived by a man she was foolish enough to have fallen in love with in one day. No one would know how pliable, gullible, and weak she is. And the disguise of anonymity would give her strength.

She makes the 1:20 to Penn Station, and Daisy works on erasing her slimy, shivery feelings about what she allowed Luke to do to her emotionally. By the time she arrives in New York, she has all but finished flogging herself and feels strong enough to permit her heart a respite in the form of remembering Luke's smile—a surprisingly shy smile that changed the self-assuredness of a handsome man into something sweet and gentle and touchable. As the train slides silently to a stop, she gives in to another vision: Luke's face, his smooth tanned skin, his soft lips so close to hers.

# CHAPTER THIRTY-SIX

Charley and Lucy are lucky. Ned Adler has come down with a terrible allergy headache and there will be no special plans. Maybe barbecue for dinner if he feels better. The kids are free to go find Daisy.

Finding anyone in Shorelane is pretty easy, even for kids without a car. Generally, people in a small blue-collar town like Shorelane don't have an unlisted number; only celebrities have to guard their privacy and as far as anyone knows, there are none in Shorelane. All Charley has to do to find Daisy Rumkin's address is look in the phone book. Turns out she lives on Maple Drive—the same street as the Duncan twins.

When Charley tells his mother he's going to play with Benny and Dennis, she says fine, but she is surprised when he says Lucy is coming with him.

"You don't have to take her," Leddy tells him privately. "I'll be home all afternoon."

But Charley says it's okay. Leddy is pleased. Ned's wrong, she thinks. Charley really doesn't mind having Lucy around.

"Be home by five in case we decide to go out to dinner," she calls after the children.

# CHAPTER THIRTY-SEVEN

Mrs. McDonnell is in her usual spot, crocheting on the front porch, when the children come up the steps. Even though she doesn't know who they are, she's happy to see them. She figures they're neighborhood children come to sell cookies or ask some questions. A lonely woman whose only daughter had long ago moved to Colorado, she is always ready for a visit.

"Hello there." She smiles. "Are you selling cookies? Raffles?"

"Uh-uh," says Charley. "We're looking for Daisy. Is she home?"

"Is Daisy a friend of yours?"

"Not exactly, but we have to ask her something."

Hungry for the company, Mrs. McDonnell isn't quick to let the children go. "Maybe I can help."

"I don't think so. Could we see Daisy?"

Now she has to tell them that Daisy isn't home and probably won't be back until tonight. "I think she went into the city."

The children stare at her blankly.

"New York."

"Oh, okay, thank you." Charley pulls his sister's arm, and they move away down the steps.

"Have you ever been to New York?" Mrs. McDonnell calls after them, but they are already far enough away to pretend they don't hear her.

"What should we do? Should we go to the beach?" Lucy asks.

"Shh. I'm thinking."

Lucy follows her brother home in silence. It's nearly four thirty. Their dad's headaches could last a few hours.

Finally, Charley tells her it's too late to go to the beach.

"When you saw him, was the blood all over, like squirting down?" he asks.

"I didn't see it squirting. It was covering his face."

"But it wasn't squirting, right? Remember that time I cut my lip on the edge of the bed? Was it squirting like that?"

"I guess not."

"Then it's probably not so bad. We'll go tomorrow, early. We won't say anything to Larry or anybody, not even Daisy, and we'll make the guy promise not to tell anyone, and if he says yes, we'll pull the stuff off him and he can go home by himself. Okay?"

"Okay. But …"

"But what?"

"He can't. He's homeless."

"Forget it, butthead."

And with that understanding, the ten-year-old and the seven-year-old comfortably decide Luke's life.

# CHAPTER THIRTY-EIGHT

Monday, July 4

Fourth of July Monday starts out sunny. Not the deep yellow sun that promises a perfect day, but a whiter, more uncertain color partially obscured by haze. Summer mornings often start with this kind of gauzy look, typically burning off before noon. A good enough day for the big picnic.

As promised, Charley and Lucy are down at the beach by eight o'clock. Charley knows that if his parents found out, he would be in terrible trouble. To say nothing of the fact that he let Lucy ride on the handlebars of his bike. But he did make her wear a helmet so maybe that would count for something.

Charley figures they would do what they have to do to free Luke, and then get right back home—maybe even in time for breakfast. The Adlers eat breakfasts late on holidays.

# CHAPTER THIRTY-NINE

By the morning of the fourth day, Luke has all but stopped trying. Like people on starvation diets who lose their appetites, his will to go on is quieting. He lies still, a lump of humanity, filthy from the stain of rat's blood, the stink of urine, and days of neglect. His face is bruised blue-black from Larry's beatings, staring dully at the piece of cement that still dangles above his head. The rats might have given rise to some fight but they haven't come back. He hasn't shouted for help in hours.

He's uncomfortable but not in great physical pain. He's still clenching and unclenching his toes to keep some circulation going in his legs. But there are no more tears. His mind has become suspended in an indistinct middle distance between clarity and obscurity. As long as everything remains calm, his thoughts stay numbed. He's sad but not in an active sense, just the drip down of defeat.

Luke hears the children coming. He doesn't want to see them.

"Hey, mister!" Charley and Lucy run into the sewer, then

stop, horrified and disgusted at the sight and stench. Charley steps back but Lucy holds her ground. Neither child is afraid. Luke's weakness is apparent even to the children.

Luke doesn't turn his head.

Charley, using every bit of humanity he knows he should feel, moves to where his sister is standing. "It's us, me and Lucy. We're gonna get the stuff off you."

"Just you?" Now Luke looks at the boy.

"No, me and my sister."

"Go away."

"We're gonna get you out," Lucy says, stepping closer to Luke. Reluctantly, Charley moves up alongside her.

"Forget it. You can't do it alone. Where are your friends?"

"We didn't tell them; Larry won't let us help you. He said we should let you die because everyone thinks you already drowned."

"Is that what you think?"

Both children shake their heads.

"That why you came here?"

Charley shrugs. "I don't know. I guess."

"So what happens when Larry finds out?"

A shadow of worry crosses Charley's face. Lucy's expression is only anger.

"I hate Larry," she says.

It's hard for Luke not to hate the whole bunch of them. But he forces himself to find some kindness, some forgiveness for these two. He tries to see them for what they are: little kids. Except for the color of their hair, he hasn't noticed what they look like. Now he sees all the details—even their freckles. Their faces are sweet and very young. Despite his hopelessness, Luke is touched that they came back all on their own. It takes courage to go up against Larry.

"It's brave what you're doing. I appreciate it."

The compliment is a surprise, and they smile at him. It's the first time he's made honest contact with any of the children.

Help has come at last, too late and too little. But despite his acute frustration with their childishness, Luke tries to remain calm and patient. Finally, he is the adult.

"I appreciate it, I do, but it's no good," he says. "You two can't lift this cement alone."

"Should we go get help?" Charley asks.

Luke doesn't bother answering. He knows Charley is too afraid of Larry. It's just an excuse to get away.

Then Lucy voices the thought for him. "Charley and me are afraid of Larry," she says.

"Am not." Charley's instant response is to defend his honor, but inside he knows she's right. He's surprised to hear that she's scared too. Like Larry, he was never sure she was.

Luke feels sorry for the kids. He remembers his own childhood bully; there's no way out of that fear except growing up. But how do you tell a kid to wait two years? Still, he tries to assuage their shame and fear, and even trying makes him feel better than he's felt in a long time.

"Sure you're scared," he says. "Who wouldn't be afraid of a bully twice your size? I remember a kid like Larry from when I was little … He made my life miserable. Years later, in my last year of high school, when I was full grown, I saw him again at a supermarket. He was a delivery boy, this sad, fat guy, and everyone was telling him what to do, even the girls at the cash register. It's a short life, being a kid bully.

"I don't know what to tell you, Charley. Just keep getting smarter, and you'll find ways to keep away from him. Look at your sister. He can't push her around and he knows it. You've got something, Lucy. Don't lose it."

The children stare at Luke in amazement, seeing him for the first time as a real person.

Even Luke sees the difference. Feels the difference.

And then Charley thinks, what if their father got trapped like Luke and nobody helped him?

"Mister?"

"Yes?"

"I'm sorry," Charley says.

And then Lucy says, "Me too."

"It was wrong what you kids did, but maybe I was wrong too."

"You didn't do anything bad," Lucy says.

"That's what I always tell myself—nothing *really* bad. But nothing really good either, and a lot of wrong. Too much wrong."

That's when the children look down then quickly step back.

"What?"

"Water," Charley says. "Look, like a little river."

"Is it raining?" Concern is back in Luke's voice.

Lucy moves to the entrance of the sewer. "Uh-uh, no," she says. "It's not raining."

"Oh shit!" This contact with the children has revitalized Luke enough for him to feel alarm. "It has to be raining someplace."

Just at that moment, thunder cracks and a heavy downpour begins. Almost instantly, the trickle of water widens to a stream, and Luke feels it bubbling up the side of his body.

"Oh God, help me, please!"

The children are horrified, instantly understanding the threat.

"Get on the other side, Luce," Charley yells, grabbing one end of the beam that runs the length of Luke's body. Lucy splashes through the rushing water to the other end, but her fingers aren't long enough to reach around. She tries to get underneath the board and shove it up with her shoulders, but it doesn't move no matter how hard she pushes. Even together the children don't have the strength to move the wood. They try to shove the cement away, but it won't budge either.

With all the fight that his newfound will to survive brings, Luke struggles to force his trapped body up against the debris. Nothing moves except the water, which keeps rising and surging.

Down on their hands and knees, the children dig and rip at the sand like frantic puppies, trying to divert the water away from Luke. The current is too strong; their channel overflows instantly. One fast torrent seizes Lucy and thrashes her against the wall of the sewer. She screams, and Charley fights through the deluge to grab her and drag her over to Luke.

They try to pull Luke by his free arm but nothing helps. Both children are crying with terror, but they don't give up.

The water mounts quickly. Now Luke can see a possible escape: if the water gets high enough to buoy the debris, the beam will be light enough for the children to move it.

No. If the water gets that deep it will be over Lucy's head. She's so small and weighs so little. She'll be washed away.

A powerful wave of determination obliterates Luke's terror, the determination not to be wrong again. He's going to die, goddamn it, he's going to die, but he's going to save these children.

"Get out of here!" he shouts. "Go! Now!"

They're too frightened and confused to move.

"Get away!" Luke shouts. "Go! Get the hell out of here!"

But they're crazed beyond sanity with the idea that they have to help free Luke. To break the spell, Luke grabs Charley by the throat and squeezes tightly, hurting him into reality.

"I'll kill you if you don't leave! Get her out of here!"

Terrified and sobbing, Charley pulls Lucy up. Dragging his sister's arm, he staggers off through the deep, rushing water into the relative safety of the storm. Outside he slips and falls; Lucy helps him up and he brushes himself off, hard. Harder than he has to.

"We're gonna get Daisy, and if we can't find her, we're gonna go to the police," he shouts.

"Okay," Lucy says.

# CHAPTER FORTY

As the water reaches Luke's face, mercifully, it falls. Not all the way, just down to his shoulders. This time the cushion stays under his head. Exhausted from terror, he rests back—

And sees Larry standing above him, pointing a gun at his head.

Luke knows instantly it's not a toy. The kid is a fucking psychopath.

"What are you doing?" he asks. His tone is quiet, almost hopeless.

"What does it look like I'm doing? I'm gonna shoot you."

"You're crazy."

"You don't have to be crazy to shoot somebody. Especially you. Nobody will care. My dad says that's why we have such big taxes, to pay for homeless bums like you. Besides, I told ya, everyone thinks you drowned anyway."

"Not the twins; they don't."

"So what? They're not gonna tell anyone if I say not to."

"Maybe not them, but what about Charley and Lucy?"

"They won't either."

"I wouldn't be so sure."

"Yeah, well, I'm sure. Ya know why?"

"Why, big shot?"

"'Cause I'm gonna kill them."

"Oh Jesus …"

"Lucy first. I don't know about Charley. There are other people I want to shoot more."

"What are you talking about?"

"The Fourth of July picnic. Everybody in Shorelane goes. All I have to do is point and shoot. I'll hit ten people with one shot. It's that crowded." Larry smiles. "I can't miss."

"Listen to me, Larry. You don't have to kill anybody. If I get out of here, I'm not going to say anything to anyone. I swear."

"No, see, I *wanna* shoot you."

"'Cause you think I'm not telling you the truth. You think I'm going to go to the police. Hey, I understand. I wasn't always honest with you, but that was before. I don't feel the same way anymore. If I say I'm not telling, I'm not telling. You can have a whole new fresh chance."

Larry considers the offer and decides against it. "Uh-uh. I'm gonna shoot you."

"Why?"

"I got my own reasons."

"No matter what it feels like this minute, I swear to you, no reason you have is good enough to kill someone. Do you have any idea what murder is? In an instant, someone's life is gone. A whole family ruined, theirs, yours, all these people destroyed forever. Maybe you're too young to understand forever."

"So what does that make me? A fuckin' moron?"

"Larry, I'm sorry. I shouldn't have said that to you. You're just a kid. I was desperate."

"A lot of people think I'm stupid, but they're all gonna be surprised. Real surprised. When you got a gun, nobody calls ya fatso or dummy or fuckin' moron."

"Yeah, maybe not when you're holding it to their heads. But you're wrong about people saying lousy things. Those people are always around. Nothing they'd like better than to ruin your life. Don't let them. It isn't worth the payback."

"Yeah, right."

"Larry. You're just a kid. What are you? Twelve? You've got a whole life ahead of you. I'll be honest: I can't like you very much. You were rotten to me, but I don't want you to die. God, in a couple of years it's all going to be so different."

"What do you know?"

"I don't know much. I wouldn't fuckin' be here if I did, but I do know that this is wrong. Okay, maybe people push you around, but you push Charley and those other kids around too. That's what happens to guys when they're young. It's bad, but you don't go killing anybody."

"Shut up."

"Why should I? You're going to kill me. I might as well say what I want."

Luke means it. He's trapped under a hundred and fifty pounds of cement and unmovable wooden beams, water creeping up to drown him, a fuckin' moron kid has a gun to his head, and he feels good.

Like a man of substance. Finally.

Look, Ma. I did get someplace.

"What's so funny?" Larry sees Luke's smile. "You think I won't shoot you?"

"Just don't hurt Lucy."

The rain has picked up, sending a new surge of water into the sewer. It laps at Luke's chin. He raises his head, extending his neck like a seagull in water.

"Maybe I won't shoot you," Larry says, toying with the gun in his hand. "Maybe I'll just let you drown. Save my bullets for extra people. Lucy."

"Please, Larry, she's just a little girl. Don't hurt her." Luke strains to turn his head, but he can no longer see Larry. Water splashes in his face, blinding him; when he opens his eyes, the sewer is empty.

"Larry!" he shouts. "Don't do it!"

The rushing water picks up one of the tools the children left behind and rides it up against Luke's body, whacking his chin and scraping across his cheek as it whips past him on the fast-moving current. He can feel debris accumulating under his feet and pieces of it knocking against his legs as the water picks up an undertow power. With each new wave, the four-by-eight beam that runs the length of his body lifts slightly for an instant and then comes down again.

He can't drown. He has to get out. He has to stop Larry!

But there's no way. He's locked in the sand. Even though the water level stays below his face, the swells splash over him, taking his breath away every time he starts to get it back. The agony of knowing that only he can save Lucy pulls at Luke's heart. Every inch of him screams out for the chance to save her, and the battle against powerlessness and death becomes so fierce that it begins to twist his trapped body into small movements.

Though the rush of water lifts the timbers only millimeters, each time it does Luke's body swells with the strength of resolution. Combined with the advantage of the current, his sand coffin spreads deeper and wider. In a moment, he's able to arch his back, allowing the water to seep under, giving him a small leeway he didn't have before. A thin branch of hope sends life to his limbs; blood and life force combine with the rush of water until Luke can wiggle one leg out from under the cement slab.

One leg free!

It takes all Luke's concentrated power to lift the limb that has atrophied into weakness after four days of movement limited to wiggling his toes. On will alone, he forces his leg up through the water, high enough to kick into the air. High enough for Luke to see his own foot for the first time in four days.

He can do it!

He must do it.

If the water were to rise just a little higher, three inches maybe, the level would be below his face but deep enough to float the wood. That's all Luke needs to scramble out from under.

If survival is the most extreme life force in nature, survival driven by the mad desire to save another life doubles its might. Luke knows he must survive or Lucy is dead. Until now, Luke has managed to avoid almost all responsibility, save those three special weeks as a kid with Spotty, the homeless dog. He did that perfectly, happily, but other demands would have been treated lackadaisically, taking the shortest cuts, often foolishly. This is the most powerful motivation he has ever had. Paradoxically, he's never felt such physical power as he feels at this very moment, trapped as he is beneath this immovable weight. For the first time in his twenty-two years, Luke may be close to understanding commitment. Perhaps, his hobbledehoyhood is truly over.

To capture a moment's respite from the pain of his precarious position, he takes a deep breath, holds it, and allows his head to rest back on the water until he must breathe again.

Still, the water doesn't mount high enough to move the beam. Minutes pass and Luke lies there, exhausted and weakening. He cannot hold this position much longer. Unless he can free himself soon, he *will* drown.

And then he hears the deluge, torrential rain pounding at the entrance to the sewer. Within seconds, a roaring torrent of water with the power of a fire hose slams into his legs, lifting first the beam, then the cement, then his whole body in its speeding torrent.

He's free!

But he's exchanged one cruel master for another. The rushing water speeds him helplessly along its course, powerful enough to drown him or carry him into the bay. He's just another piece of debris riding the powerful chaos. Lost in the rush, there's still time for jubilation, foolish or not. He's going to make it! He's going to save that little girl!

And then something huge and dark, the freed four-by-eight, whacks into the side of his skull, right at eye level, snapping his head back. Colored lights explode in lines and circles across his field of vision.

The beam slams him again. And the lights go black.

# CHAPTER FORTY-ONE

The rain let up briefly, but now it's coming down in sheets. Charley, with Lucy squeezed onto the bar between the seat and the handlebars, peddles with all his strength toward Daisy's house.

They ride through puddles so deep that wings of water cascade into the air on either side of the bike. Charley doesn't slow down. He has to get to Daisy or Luke is going to drown. He saw how fast the water could turn into a dangerous river; he watched it pick up his sister and throw her against the wall. Pinned the way Luke was, Charley knew there was nothing he could do to free him.

At Daisy's, Charley skids to a stop; Lucy slides down and he lets the bike fall. The two children speed up the front steps onto the porch, and Charley leans on the doorbell until Mrs. McDonnell appears.

"My goodness," Mrs. McDonnell says. "Daisy's friends. It's so nice to see you again."

"Could we see Daisy, please?" Charley asks.

"But you're soaking wet. What are you doing out in such rain?"

"Please, ma'am, we have to talk to Daisy."

"First thing you have to do is come inside. It's just too nasty out there."

"*Please*, ma'am." Lucy is close to tears. "We need Daisy right away."

The naturally loquacious and hopelessly friendly Mrs. Mc-Donnell sees the children's urgency and puts aside her desire for conversation to go find Daisy.

"We'll just say that man got caught in the sewer and he asked us to get her," Charley whispers to Lucy.

Lucy agrees, and when Daisy comes down the stairs that's just what Charley says—except he adds that the sewer was on the beach where Daisy had been the other night.

The children watch Daisy's face go white. "He's alive?"

They nod. Daisy begins to cry.

"Oh, thank God! Thank God he's not dead!"

Charley and Lucy back away, overwhelmed by her reaction. Even Mrs. McDonnell is surprised. As a tenant, Daisy has always been polite and quiet; she certainly never showed even a hint of this sort of emotion. Completely confused, Mrs. McDonnell asks the children if they were talking about a relative, and they both shrug.

Between sobs, Daisy tells her that Luke isn't a relative, just a good friend. Remembering her story to Lucy, she adds, "An old, good friend."

Before she can continue, Lucy speaks up, tiny hands clasped tightly together.

"He's gonna drown if you don't get there really fast."

The gravity in the little girl's voice registers.

"Come on," Daisy says. "Show me where he is."

"Can you take your car?" Charley asks.

Daisy shakes her head. She doesn't have a car. Neither does Mrs. McDonnell.

"Then you can take my bike. Lucy and I can walk home."

Daisy stands, paralyzed, her own ambivalence about Luke further complicating the children's unsatisfactory explanation of what happened to him. It was all too much, too fast—but in the face of the children's panic, everything boiled down to: "Yes, I will." Without bothering to put on a raincoat, Daisy rushes outside.

"It's the rain sewer right where you were ..." Charley fumbles for the right explanation. "Where you were."

Daisy vanishes before he can finish, jumping on the bike and shouting back over her shoulder, "I'll return it later! Thank you!"

Charley and Lucy stand in the rain, watching Daisy speed off. In that moment, they have no doubt that Luke will be saved.

They feel pretty okay. Like Luke said, brave.

# CHAPTER FORTY-TWO

Everything in Shorelane closes for the holiday, including the bars. That means John O'Neill will be home all morning. Larry keeps to his room, waiting until his mother goes into the kitchen to make breakfast. Larry won't eat until his father finishes.

If Mr. O'Neill had a long night, it will be a quick breakfast. A long night either in a bar or in the living room drinking Irish alone, listening to Ted Nugent, and falling asleep on the couch.

Larry knows today will be a fast breakfast. He heard at least four repeats of "Sweet Sally" last night when he was trying to sleep.

He waits and listens.

His father is shouting at his mother. Larry can't hear her responses, but even on the rare occasions when she makes one, it's always so soft you can hardly hear it. It doesn't make any difference anyway; Mr. O'Neill never listens to his wife.

Larry wishes his father was dead a thousand times every day. Except sometimes, just before John O'Neill gets mean drunk, in that strange middle between sobriety and the cusp of inebriation, there is a loosening, a brief moment of affection for whoever is near. Larry has seen him grab out for his wife and hug her, though she is always too nervous to enjoy it. Larry has also seen him slide his hand under her skirt. That's when Larry disappears, runs up to hide in his room.

Other times Larry is the nearest. And then John O'Neill will put his hand on the boy's shoulder and pull him close. While Larry is never unafraid of his father, he can't help but respond to the feel of so much strong, warm body against his own.

But the affection only lasts until the next drink takes John O'Neill back to his true self, and that's bad, 'cause his father is a big man, tall, like Luke, and powerful. Luke would be powerful too, if he was free. And he'd be sore at Larry, like his father is always pissed off at him for something, though half the time Larry doesn't even know what he did. Because mostly it was nothing. But with Luke, he would know.

It is rare for the boy to have physical contact with another human being outside of a fight with one of the little kids. Even when he touches someone, it's never affectionate. When he was little, when his father wasn't around, his mother would hold him. As he got older, even that contact diminished—a quick touch, a hand on his back to lead him to the table or straighten his jacket. Now she almost never touches him.

Larry knows it's because he grew up so ugly. Fatso, creep, sweatball, all the things the kids call him, they're all true; that's why his mother doesn't like him anymore.

He's only twelve. But he's a twelve-year-old with a gun. That's going to make a difference to everyone. They'll see.

It makes Larry smile. Nobody has any idea what he's planning. Nobody even suspects. But by the end of the day, everybody in Shorelane will be talking. He'll be the most important kid around.

And when the television crews come, everyone will say dumb things like, "Oh, he was just an ordinary kid. He didn't look like he would shoot anybody. Where did he get the gun anyway?"

Maybe they'll arrest his father because it was his gun.

Whatever happens, thanks to Larry O'Neill, this will be a Fourth of July no one will ever forget.

The guy in the sewer, he knows what's going to happen. He might have tried to stop Larry, but he's dead, drowned. So that's okay.

Larry plans it out in his head, how it's going to look.

Lucy will definitely be first. Then that asshole Ryan from next door. After that it's up for grabs. Anybody will do. Plenty of guys from his class will be there.

Suddenly, Larry has a great idea—how about one of the twins? They're always hanging around him; they'll be real close. And the beauty of it: it doesn't even matter which one he shoots.

Larry hears his father going up the stairs. It's now safe to go to the kitchen.

Nonetheless, he goes very quietly.

Carol O'Neill is waiting for her son. Normally, she would have made pancakes because she knows they're Larry's favorite and she likes to make them. But this morning's argument with John has unnerved her. She knows she has to go up and apologize. If she doesn't, he'll spend all day nursing his grievances and all night drinking them into a full-blown fury. So instead of the pancakes Larry loves, it's cold cereal.

She is setting the bowl at Larry's place when he comes into the kitchen.

"You can have Total or that new cereal with the raisins if you want," she says.

"Total's okay," Larry says. "Is Dad going to the picnic?"

Larry hopes he isn't. It will be hard to shoot anybody in front of his dad. He'll be embarrassed—and scared.

"Not now, maybe later. I'll probably stay home and keep him company."

The thought of keeping John O'Neill company is ludicrous, but what else can she say?

"Can I go?" her son asks.

It's always better to have Larry out of the house on the weekends when John is home. No matter what Larry's mother does, there's always trouble. John just finds it. Or makes it.

"Of course you can go." She dries her hands on a dish towel. "I'm going to make the beds. Put your bowl in the sink when you're finished, and don't forget to put the butter away."

She folds the dish towel and puts it on the rack next to the sink. "If Dad decides to go to the picnic later, we'll find you."

She leaves Larry alone in the kitchen. He prays his father won't change his mind. He probably won't. John O'Neill doesn't like social events.

Larry eats his cereal, finds two doughnuts from yesterday, eats them, and scoops out some peanut butter, eating it with his fingers. Finally, he wipes his hand, pats the gun in his pocket, and leaves.

He forgets to put the butter away.

* * *

Next door, Ryan is getting ready to pick up Ashley for the picnic. He sees Larry leaving. He could give him a lift, but the thought of that kid sweating up the upholstery in his dad's car turns him off. Besides, he can't have a little creep like that around Ashley. She might think they're friends or something.

Ryan waits until Larry is halfway down the street before he gets in the car.

# CHAPTER FORTY-THREE

Charley and Lucy are overjoyed to see the sun. Not only does it mean Luke is probably okay, surely okay, it means the picnic is on. Next to Christmas, this is the most exciting day of the year.

They want Daisy to save Luke, but they don't really want to see either of them ever again. They just want it all to be over.

"Do you think Daisy'll bring Luke to the picnic?" Lucy asks. "Do you think he told on us?"

The thought almost ruins the picnic for Charley. That—and seeing Larry. But of course, Larry won't know they told Daisy. But what if Luke really does come and he sees them? What if he sees Larry? Suddenly the picnic seems like a terrible idea.

"I'm not going," he says to Lucy.

His mother overhears as she comes into the room. "Where are you not going?" she asks.

"To the picnic."

"Are you sick?"

"Yeah, my stomach …"

"Let me take your temperature. When did this start?"

"Me, too," Lucy says. "My stomach hurts too."

It isn't easy to fool Leddy Adler. She knows her children too well.

"Okay," she asks, "what's up?"

"Nothing," they say at the same time.

Hitting pretty near the bull's-eye, she asks, "Is it that awful O'Neill kid? I'm talking to your father about him. We're going to have a word with his dad." She goes to the foot of the steps to call her husband, who's already on his way downstairs dressed in jeans and a T-shirt for the picnic.

Ned Adler is slim and more boyish than his early forties age would indicate and red-haired like both his children. When Leddy tells him why the children don't want to go to the picnic, her voice is almost shaking with anger.

"We have to do something about that kid, Ned." She turns to Charley. "Charley, I told you not to play with him. He's too old to be hanging around with ten-year-olds anyway."

"What is it, Charley?" Ned asks. "Is he pushing you around again?"

Of course, both children shake their heads vehemently. Their father, unconvinced, turns to Lucy. Lucy is the kind of child who rarely makes excuses. She tells the straight truth and whatever happens, happens.

"Lucy, is it—what's his name? The O'Neill kid?"

The little girl hesitates, looking at Charley. "Yeah … yeah, we don't like him."

"Okay, but you can't let him keep you away from things you want to do. And, Charley, you can't be afraid all the time. Tell you what: you find that kid and tell him that if he bothers you or your sister again, your father is going to take it up with his father."

"Larry's really afraid of his dad," Charley says.

"With good reason. His father is a goddamn bully too. But don't worry, I'm not really going to say anything to John O'Neill. I think the threat will be enough to stop Larry."

"I'm for actually talking to his father," Leddy says. "I've had enough of that kid."

"I can't do that, Leddy. The kid may be a bully, but he's not dangerous. John O'Neill, now he can be one out-of-control guy. I remember him from school. Even then he had a bad temper, especially when he drank, and he drinks plenty now. I'd be scared to say something, not for myself, but for his kid."

Reluctantly, Leddy agrees.

"Charley," Ned says. "You have to do this on your own or you'll never get rid of him. I can give you the weapon, but you have to use it. Okay?"

"Okay," Lucy says, answering for her brother. "We'll do it."

"Not you!" Leddy says. "You keep away from that boy."

Lucy nods, but she doesn't mean it. She'll stick with Charley. She knows he needs her help.

\* \* \*

At the Duncan house, the twins have been up and ready since eight. Their mother insisted that the pouring rain meant there wouldn't be a picnic, but when it begins to clear around ten, they start nagging, and around ten thirty she finally says they can go.

They are in a hurry to find Larry before Charley arrives. They don't want to share their best friend with anybody.

At no time during the morning do they talk about the man in the sewer. If they think about Luke at all, neither mentions it. Anticipation of the Fourth of July festivities has taken over all their thoughts.

# CHAPTER FORTY-FOUR

It takes less than ten minutes for Daisy to arrive at the parking lot above the beach. In that time, the sun has come out blazing, the shrubs and sand absorbing all trace of the storm in minutes. Only Daisy, with her dripping hair and soaking clothes, provides evidence of the downpour that took place.

Daisy rides through the little lakes of rainwater to the edge of the dunes. There, she abandons the bike and hurries to the top of the sand hill. Scrambling over the plastic fence, now flattened by the heavy rain, she slides on the back of her heels down the steep slope. Wasting no time looking around, she heads for the sewer.

It's empty.

Except for a large beam rammed up against the wall, she sees nothing unusual there. At her feet a thin rivulet of water runs from somewhere back in the darkness, winding its way toward the mouth of the sewer, heading in the direction of the bay but never making it out onto the beach.

"Luke! Luke!" Daisy calls out.

Only her echo answers.

Why did she believe those kids? Of course he isn't here. What an idiot she was to fall for a trick like that. They must have been laughing themselves sick at the way she took off on the bike. Serves them right if she doesn't return it.

Yet something isn't right. Daisy doesn't know Lucy that well, but she's sure this wouldn't be her kind of trick. Larry maybe, but not Lucy. She and Charley seemed genuinely upset too.

Maybe Larry scared them into doing it.

Of course.

Daisy sits down on the beam, her world shattered once again.

Luke drowned. He lied, and then he drowned. That's it. She has to accept it. But for a moment, back at the house, she thought her heart would burst with joy. That blinding flash of happiness made her feel incandescent. From that brief instant until now, in the time it took her to realize the truth, Luke was alive. She would see him again. She wanted so much to see him again.

It's cool and peaceful in the sewer, but that's no comfort to Daisy. The pain in her chest cuts her breath into short gasps; she's overheated, almost too dizzy to stand. After a few minutes, knowing it's not going to get better, she decides to go home.

Outside, the sight of sunlight tripping on the water and the soft cool breeze gives Daisy back her breath. With the tide out, the beach is as wide as it can be, stretching more than a hundred feet into the distance. Daisy can see sailboats racing in circles far out on the bay. Other than the call of seagulls, it's quiet. Everyone in Shorelane is at the picnic.

Daisy's eyes, sweeping aimlessly along the shore, stop on what looks like a pile of clothes. It's far out, at the edge where sand meets water. She watches for a moment, decides maybe it's just some rocks, and turns to go.

After a few steps, she turns back and starts walking toward the sea.

Then she starts running.

# CHAPTER FORTY-FIVE

Luke's foot is trapped, twisted and squeezed into the small opening of the pipe. No matter how hard he fights, the suction holding him is too great, and there is nothing to grab onto to give him leverage. Water swirls around him like heavy air, thick but strangely breathable, black with tiny particles of white dust too dense to see through. When Luke holds his hand to his face, he can make out the dim outline of his fingers. Beyond that, nothing.

Even though he isn't choking on the water, he feels an enormous urgency to break through the surface into the air. But his foot is stuck fast.

Something cold touches his head, then clamps on and begins to pull him. His foot snaps free of the pipe and he moves upward at a great speed, so great that he feels the whoosh of air spinning his stomach over and over. Finally, it slows, the air becoming lighter in weight and color as he nears what feels like the surface.

Now the touch on his head is softer, the cold only cool and

the feel more like a caress. With great effort, Luke reaches out to return the gentle touch moving lightly across his forehead. Luke opens his eyes and sees Daisy, lovely Daisy, leaning over him, so close that her hair tickles his face.

He closes his eyes again to enjoy more of the dream, but the inside of his eyelids is empty of Daisy. Only the brightness of the sun, trying to peek in at the corners, is visible.

A shadow softens the sun and Luke opens his eyes again. There she is. What a beautiful dream. The sweet face with sunlight haloing her hair.

"Luke."

He can even hear her soft whispery voice.

"Luke. Are you all right?"

He opens his eyes and a blinding pain shoots through his head with such ferocity that he squeezes his eyes shut to close it out.

The touch is on his forehead again. This time he can feel fingers; his dream Daisy is running her soft hand over his face.

"Luke, can you speak? Talk to me."

In his dream, he opens his mouth, but no sound comes out. Pain rips through his jaw; he grimaces.

"It's all right," Daisy says. "You've been hurt, but it's okay. It's stopped bleeding."

There is something so sensible and ordinary about her words and such a reality to the sound of her voice that Luke's dreamlike state is shaken. Logic intrudes: dare he hope that it isn't a dream? That somehow, miraculously, he has been saved? That he's alive?

Of course he's alive. Dead people don't dream.

He opens his eyes and sees that it *is* Daisy, flesh-and-blood Daisy. He could weep, he's so overjoyed. He couldn't be any happier if he loved her.

Daisy smiles, and though there is still concern in her face, the smile is joyful. "You didn't drown."

Luke tries to smile back but it hurts too much. Tears fill his eyes and begin to trickle down his cheeks. Daisy wipes them away.

\* \* \*

Daisy looks down at Luke, taking in his growth of blond beard and his terribly bruised face, all washed clean like a stone rubbed shiny by the sea. She puts her head on his chest and smells the saltwater. He wraps his arms around her and holds her tight.

They stay like that for a long time. A perfect fit. Old friends, lovers … the only two people in the world.

\* \* \*

With his arms around Daisy, her head still resting on his chest, Luke begins to tell her the horror of his four days trapped in the sewer. Not the rats or the kids or the water, he skims over that, but the horror of realizing he'd wasted his life and knowing that knowledge was too late coming to count.

Then he tells her about the children. Again, not about the terrible things they did, only that they saw his worthlessness and reflected it back at him.

He tells her how he lied to her. Without making excuses, he tells her how ashamed he is. And then something escapes from his heart and falls into words so quickly, so unexpectedly, that he himself hears it for the first time.

"I love you," he says.

And it's true. An enormous, world-shaking, terrifying emotion reduced to three words. He just does. Simple as that. He feels the purity of it cleansing his sins.

Daisy lifts her head and looks at him, waiting for the caveat: he loves her … for finding him, saving him, for whatever good deed she has done. But she can see in his face and feel in his arms that this love is not gratitude. It's that same foolish, inexplicable, overwhelming feeling she has had since the first time she met him.

Perhaps Daisy loved the old Luke foolishly, but this man, this man reborn is different. She can feel it.

Gently, taking care not to touch his bruises, Daisy kisses Luke. It's only a whisper of a kiss, one that barely touches his lips, yet in it he feels his love returned.

Her kiss gives him the courage to tell her the other things that happened. The children's cruelty, his shame and degradation, the rats, the blood, the river of rain, everything he can remember about the devastation of those four days.

But his memory is incomplete. The blow from the beam confused the moments just before and during the rainstorm, and Luke grows more and more unsettled. He knows something happened, something important, but he's unable to dig it out. Desperate urgency rises within him.

Daisy listens in horror. "Please, Luke, no more." She helps him to his feet. Unsteady, he leans on her, too weak to do anything but stand. "You're hurt. We have to get you to a hospital. Can you walk?"

Luke stands with one arm on Daisy's shoulder, breathing deeply, allowing most of his 160-pound weight to be supported by the slender young woman.

Daisy holds onto him, her heels digging into the sand. If he's too heavy, she doesn't show it. She waits patiently for him to gather enough strength to take a step.

He does. Unsteady, knees nearly buckling, but through the force of their shared determination, they find the strength to keep him upright. In this halting, painful way, they struggle across the beach toward the dunes. Even through the pain and weakness, Luke feels something powerful scratching at the back of his brain, pressing hard enough to send darts of panic through his whole body. He can feel it but he can't read it.

Daisy sees his anxiety. "It's all right, Luke. We're not in a hurry. No one's around. Even the doctor will be at the picnic."

"Picnic?" The word is important, but he doesn't know why.

"The Fourth of July picnic. Big doings in Shorelane."

Daisy chatters on, trying to calm Luke with descriptions of the town's holiday festivities. But Luke doesn't hear her.

*Picnic. Picnic. Picnic.*

He uses the word to wrench out the locked thoughts torturing his memory. "Picnic," he repeats. There's something there, but he just can't find it.

Later, he tells himself, when he's calm. It will come to him. The decision allows Luke to relax somewhat, and in that moment, as he loosens his mind, the memory comes rushing back like the torrent of water that nearly drowned him.

Larry. The gun.

"Lucy!" A surge of adrenaline courses through Luke's body. "That son-of-a-bitch Larry is going to shoot Lucy!"

His shout comes out at full strength, adrenaline whipping him past his infirmity and filling his veins with the power he thought he'd lost. "Daisy, we have to get there!"

The man who moments ago could barely stand charges across the dunes. Falling, standing, scrambling, and falling again and raking the sand to stand up, but always rushing forward, charging on!

Daisy races behind him, shouting questions. "What do you mean, Luke? What are you talking about?"

Luke is running too hard to answer.

"I have a bike!" Daisy shouts.

"No good! Over there!" Luke points to a beat-up Volkswagen on the street across from the beach parking lot. Daisy runs after him.

The car door is unlocked. The advantage of small-town living.

Inside of two minutes, Luke has hotwired the car—the advantage of big city life—and they're following Daisy's instructions to the picnic grounds.

# CHAPTER FORTY-SIX

The day has cleared brilliantly, splendid weather for a wonderful Fourth of July picnic. On the picnic grounds in Shorelane Park, people are already gathering as if they were waiting around the bend in a sprinter's crouch for the weather to clear. Cars and trucks loaded with festive paraphernalia are unloading in the parking lot. Despite the wet earth, people are setting up booths on the football field in front of an antique carousel gifted to the town by a wealthy former resident some sixty years ago. It hasn't worked in fifty, but they put it up every year anyway. It's tradition. On the far side, men are just finishing assembling a wooden bandstand.

All of Shorelane loves this picnic, even people who don't like Shorelane. It feels like an old-fashioned Technicolor musical about small-town holidays somewhere in the innocent, nameless middle of the country; indeed, with the band pumping out old favorites, all it needs is Judy Garland.

Even though the music is persistently old-fashioned, the younger kids love it. The teenagers are another story. Usually they bring their own music and make their own party off in a corner on the basketball court.

For the first time ever, Shorelane has rented a carnival setup for the Fourth of July. It's got bumper cars on one side and a kiddy ride on the other. It isn't even eleven o'clock, and there are already long lines for both.

The traveling carnival company is a little tired and shabby, but it has its own refreshment stands with cotton candy, zeppoli, and all the usual sodas, popcorn, and hot dogs. There's a shooting gallery, basketball hoops, and a wheel of fortune with a live fortune teller. This is easily Shorelane's biggest, most extravagant Fourth of July picnic ever, and the minute the sun came out, the crowds began to arrive. Nearly a thousand people are expected, an enormous turnout for a town of Shorelane's size.

The Adler family arrives early so Charley and Lucy can ride the bumper cars before the line is too long, but to Ned and Leddy's surprise neither child wants to go on the ride. Instead, Charley wheedles permission to go off on his own. He plans to find a safe place to hide. Lucy will have to stay with her parents.

"Now set your watch, Charley," says Leddy. "We'll meet back in front of the bumper cars at twelve. Make sure you're on time."

"Can't I go with Charley?" Lucy asks.

"No, honey," says her mother. "It's too crowded; you'll get lost with all these people."

"Let her go, Leddy," Ned Adler says with a smile. Like her son, Leddy is in charge of all the family worrying. She worries too much, and her husband worries too little. "It's only an hour, and she'll be with Charley. Right, Lucy? You'll stay with your brother?"

"I promise," says Lucy.

Leddy is unconvinced, but she has to admit that this year

Charley has proven to be much more responsible than she expected. He's done an excellent job taking care of Lucy—except for that one little lapse in going down to the beach. Besides, this is a family event and the Adlers know most of the people here.

"Okay, but if you two are a minute late, we're taking you straight home. Got that?"

Lucy nods enthusiastically, and Charley says, "Okay." He could do without the company, but he isn't about to cross Lucy. Not now.

"And stay away from that O'Neill kid, you hear?" Ned says. The warning is unnecessary: Charley and Lucy have every intention of staying as far away from Larry, Benny, and Dennis as possible.

In fact, it's Charley's plan to keep away from the main part of the picnic just in case Daisy and that guy show up. They're convinced Daisy saved him.

No matter how fabulous the picnic promises to be, it would never be good this year for either of the Adler children.

With Charley in the lead, the two children go straight to the basketball court where the teenagers hang out. They know they're safe there; Larry will never show up there. He hates kids his own age or older, and they don't like him very much either. The ones in his class are always making fun of him and calling him Sweatball.

No danger, Charley's sure of it. Larry will stay far away from the basketball court.

* * *

The twins have been at the picnic for almost twenty minutes, but they still haven't found Larry. He isn't at the bumper cars or any of the booths. They search everywhere they can think of before finally deciding he hasn't arrived. Maybe he isn't even coming.

"No way," Benny tells Dennis. They've been talking about the picnic for weeks. Larry has a great plan where they set up their own Three Card Monte table and make tons of money. Larry knows how to do everything.

It's always fun to be with Larry. They do crazy things, like exploring places Benny and Dennis would never go on their own. Like, they would never have gone down to the beach without Larry, and they'd never have found the sewer and done that stuff with the homeless guy. It was fantastic, like owning their own person. He was a grown-up, but it didn't matter; they could do anything they want with him.

And if some of the stuff Larry dreams up isn't so fun, you gotta figure he still knows what he's doing. He's twelve. If he says it's okay, it's okay. Right?

Neither twin speaks to the other about the crying times with Larry. If you want to have a big kid as a best friend, that's the way it has to be.

They're disappointed when they don't find him. Here they are in the middle of the biggest picnic Shorelane has ever had and they have nothing to do.

\* \* \*

The twins can't find Larry because he isn't on the lawn. He's in the wooded area on the hillside above, scoping out his killing field.

# CHAPTER FORTY-SEVEN

The "wooded area" isn't actually big enough to qualify as woods, being just a football field–sized stand of trees on top of a hillside, but the ground underneath is untended and rugged, giving it the appearance of a miniature forest. A narrow dry riverbed bordered by little cliffs of rocks runs through the middle and drops down almost six feet on either side. Where it reaches the edge of the hillside, it has been filled in with earth.

From the outside, the woods look dense, but from inside looking out, the picnic area, the carnival setup, the basketball court, and the parking lot are all clearly visible. It isn't even noon yet, and the lot is almost full, rows of cars shimmering in the sunshine.

Larry leans against a tree. He's overheated, his face blotchy red from running through the parking lot, ducking down behind cars, and trying to keep low in case the twins or Charley are around. He doesn't care about other people; they won't look at him anyway. But he doesn't want his entourage to see him until he's ready.

He has a plan. He's going to get Lucy to come back into the woods with him where nobody can see, and he's going to shoot her. After that, he'll go out and do the real stuff in front of everybody.

Won't they just shit in their pants when he starts shooting?

Maybe he can get the twins and Ryan and Charley and some of the kids in his class together and *bam-bam-bam*, get as many as he can. He'll have five bullets left after Lucy; if they're close enough together, he can't miss. But he'll have to arrange it.

Getting the twins and Charley'll be easy. They'll do whatever he says. He could tell the others that Ryan has something to show them. They'll go because everybody likes Ryan—he's a big-shot basketball player. Yeah, he'll work it around Ryan.

But first he has to get Lucy.

It won't be easy. She won't go anyplace alone with him, and he can't trick her—she'll just stare at him in that creepy way she has. The only way is to scare the shit out of her.

But it's not like with the twins; Lucy doesn't get that kind of scared. Maybe if he tells her Charley is hurt or bleeding or something? He'll get Charley away from her long enough to say he got hurt.

Except she's always sticking to Charley like glue.

Fuck, Larry hates her.

\* \* \*

When Larry steps out of the woods, he sees the twins near the shooting gallery. They don't see him. Good, he doesn't want them now. Later, maybe. They can stay with Charley while he kills Lucy.

Exhilaration shoots through Larry, making him smile. It's like he's making a movie the way he's arranging everything. And he's the star. He's the one doing the killing. That's the guy everybody watches: the guy with the gun.

After today, Larry O'Neill is all anybody in Shorelane's gonna talk about. For years they're gonna shiver and say, "Remember Larry O'Neill, the guy who shot all those kids at the picnic?" And then they'll say where they were when he was shooting and they'll be so full of it, talking about how they just missed getting shot or how they grabbed this kid and saved him, bullshit like that.

They'll remember how one minute O'Neill was just standing there all regular-like and the next second he had a gun and everyone was screaming and running and falling to the ground but it didn't matter. He'd kill five people, one with each bullet. And maybe even more because sometimes, like they said about President Kennedy in history class, one bullet gets two guys.

And then they'll say how cool he was, how he wasn't nervous at all. He just stood there and didn't say anything as he pumped out the bullets. *Bam—bam—bam.*

They'll talk about this day forever. They'll make a movie out of it. Maybe I'll even get to see it, Larry thinks. I'd like someone cool to play me. Like Harry Styles; girls love him.

In the movie, they'll show the truth, that if they didn't treat me so lousy, I wouldn't have gotten mad.

They'll see it was mostly their fault. But before all of that: Lucy.

Larry smiles. Lucy is gonna die. He's gonna shoot her in the head.

Or maybe in her ear, 'cause what if she moves while he's got the gun pointed at her head? He might miss. Maybe he should have practiced someplace first. Missing and wasting bullets could ruin everything.

Larry's only got six and if he doesn't kill enough people, it might not even get on television.

Nope. He's not taking any chances. He's gonna do it in her ear so that even if she does move, the gun will stay stuck in there.

She's probably gonna scream. He's gotta make sure to get his hand over her mouth first. But she's such a little shit she'll probably bite him. No good. He's gotta find another way to keep her quiet. In the movies, the guy always hits the victim in the head with the gun. Pistol-whipped; he's seen it a million times.

So, say she's following him into the woods. He stops short and spins around quickly; she'll be surprised, and before she can say anything, he'll smack her right across the face with the gun. That'll knock her out. Then he can shoot her anyplace. But maybe he should stick to shooting her in the ear? Or even better, right between the eyes. That's another expression he remembers from television. It must work. They wouldn't say it if it wasn't true.

# CHAPTER FORTY-EIGHT

On the way to the basketball court, Charley and Lucy see the twins standing by the shooting gallery. They duck around the back hoping to miss them, but the twins are like one person with four eyes. It's Benny who spots Lucy.

"Hey, where's your brother?"

"Home," she says, but Dennis catches Charley on the other side of the booth. All he wants to know is, where's Larry?

"I don't know," Charley says, thankful Larry isn't there. "C'mon," he says to Lucy.

"Where ya goin'?" Benny asks.

"No place," Charley says and keeps walking.

"Okay," Benny says, pulling his brother by the arm. "We'll go with you."

# CHAPTER FORTY-NINE

From the edge of the woods, looking down from the top of the hillside, Larry sees the four kids walking in the direction of the basketball court. That's bad luck, them going there. That's where his tormentors, the teenagers, hang out. He makes it a practice to stay as far away from them as possible.

Although today, when he's ready to start shooting, he'd like to find some of them.

Larry ducks back into the woods and cuts around to the basketball side to keep a check on the kids. To his surprise, the court is empty except for a lone girl sitting on the grass smoking.

Larry heads down to the court, walking fast. The big kids could be back any minute. He's gotta get Charley away quickly.

"Hey, Charley!" he shouts as he closes the distance between the woods and the court. The run is sharply downhill and takes him faster than his overweight body can comfortably accommodate. He's nearly sliding, on the edge of tripping, hoping that the gun in his pocket doesn't fire and blow his balls off.

\* \* \*

"Should we go back to Mommy?" Lucy whispers to Charley. Her brother keeps watching the advancing Larry, trying to figure out if it's a good "Hey, Charley!" or a bad one. It sounds okay. Larry doesn't look angry. Maybe he doesn't know about them going to see Luke and sending Daisy to help him.

The twins are overjoyed to see Larry. Now the action can begin.

"We were lookin' all over for you," says Benny.

"Where were you?" adds Dennis.

Both of them are jumping all over him like puppies.

But Larry pays no attention to them.

"Charley, come with me. I wanna show you something."

"What about us?" Benny wants to know.

"I'll show you right after. C'mon, Charley, it's gonna be gone if we don't hurry."

"Why can't we come too?" A whine is starting in Dennis's voice.

"You gotta stay with Lucy. Shut up; I'll be right back."

"Lucy has to come with me," Charley says.

"Just leave her here for a minute. She shouldn't see this."

"How come?" Lucy wants to know.

Larry whispers something in Charley's ear that Charley can't quite hear. Something about a cut-off dick.

"Wait here," Charley tells Lucy. "I'll be right back."

"C'mon!" Larry is already running up the hill toward the woods, Charley close behind him.

"What did he say?" Benny asks Lucy.

She shrugs. "I don't know. All I heard was something like a cut-off dick."

"No shit!" both twins say in unison.

# CHAPTER FIFTY

On the far side of the picnic grounds, Luke skids the car to a stop. He and Daisy jump out. Luke is still unsteady on his feet, but he's using every bit of his strength to charge ahead, clumsy and ungainly, but moving fast. They both dive right into the middle of the crowd.

"You take that side," Luke calls, "and we'll meet up at the end near those booths."

"Right," Daisy says. Neither of them considers how disreputable and out-of-place Luke looks. How unlike the happy groups of clean, crisply dressed suburbanites he is, with his bruised, swollen face accentuated by a four-day growth of beard, his wild and messy hair, torn jeans, and bare feet. And the fact that he's running through a crowd that's leisurely milling.

Almost instantly, he's noticed. The response that follows in his wake is hostile. But Luke picks his way so quickly through the clots of people, head bobbing back and forth in search of Lucy, that he's gone before anyone can stop him. But as he passes through the crowd, each person stops and turns his head, trying to follow the stranger.

Luke doesn't even look at their faces as he whips past, his eyes focused downward, searching for the little girl. He's not aware of the commotion he is causing until someone grabs his arm.

"Hold on there!" A burly, beer-bellied hulk stops him.

Luke tries to free himself, but the man's grasp is like iron.

"Let me go. I have to find someone. It's a matter of life and death."

The minute Luke says the words, he regrets them. The fact that they're true doesn't alter the fact that they sound so bizarrely melodramatic. That attitude, combined with his appearance, makes the situation even worse.

"Who the fuck are you?"

"It doesn't matter. There's a little girl in danger and I have to find her."

"Yeah, I know, life and death. You don't belong here."

By now, an unfriendly crowd has materialized around Luke.

"Who is he?" someone asks, and someone else answers, "Some kind of nut."

"Hey! I know that guy. He lifted a bottle of vodka from my store! He's a thief! Lemme at that son of a bitch!"

The big man holding Luke twists Luke's arm behind his back. The barman grabs his legs, and they start pulling him to the ground.

"Watch out! He's crazy!" someone shouts. Luke fights, but the more he struggles, the more people jump in to restrain him. Finally, buried under a mountain of men and women, Luke's fragile strength is exhausted. He's physically overwhelmed.

But still he shouts, "Let me go! I have to find her!"

It's no use. He's powerless, trapped under the weight of flesh and bone that holds him as fast as the beams and concrete of his sewer prison. Once again, he's an impotent, a homeless man, a drifter, a bum, the nonperson to whom the children reduced him.

"Daisy! Daisy!" he shouts. His last chance, but there's no way she can hear him through the noise of a thousand people enjoying a carnival picnic.

# CHAPTER FIFTY-ONE

Charley follows Larry through the picnic area to the parking lot.

"C'mon." Larry motions to Charley, pointing to a black SUV. "Get behind that car."

"What for?"

"Ya wanna see the dick?"

"Yeah."

"Well, ya gotta wait here. I gotta find out if they'll let you." Larry is dancing on the balls of his feet, practically bristling with energy. "I'll be right back," he says and takes off.

Obediently, Charley waits, adjusting himself to hide from the sun. He watches Larry head back in the direction they came from.

Weird, a cut-off dick. Probably from some kind of animal, but Larry made it sound like it was human. Holy shit, what if it was from Luke? What if Larry went back before Daisy got there?

Larry's crazy. He could do something like that.

Now Charley doesn't want to be here. He checks his watch.

It's almost eleven thirty. If he's not back by twelve his mother is going to have a fit. They'll have to leave the picnic. That would solve everything. He'll wait another ten minutes, then go back, get Lucy, and tell Larry his mother is waiting.

# CHAPTER FIFTY-TWO

The three children watch the teenage girl sitting alongside the basketball court smoking. It's weed; they can smell it. The girl smokes slowly, and when the joint is too small to hold, she wets her fingers, squeezes it out, and puts it carefully in the breast pocket of her jean jacket. Then she lies back on the grass to better enjoy the lovely float.

The twins are pretending to be high from her secondhand smoke.

Lucy watches them twirling crazily across the court, laughing, falling down, and crawling as if they can't get to their feet. She moves back out of their dust to the small circle of shade by the basketball hoop and watches the hillside for Charley.

From time to time Lucy turns back to the twins, observing them with the same kind of detached interest a person would use to watch two dogs playing. For Lucy, there's always something animal-like about the twins, like pets who do what they're told.

Except animals are cuter.

In all the time she's known Benny and Dennis, she's never

heard them talk normally to anyone. Larry tells them what to do and they do it, no matter how dumb it is. And they agree, over and over, just agree with anything Larry says. Lucy wonders if they ever talk regularly to each other. What if they get married and have children? Will Larry still tell them what to do?

At that moment, Lucy hears Larry calling her name. "Lucy! C'mere, quick! Charley's bleeding! Hurry!"

Without a word, Lucy takes off up the hill, the twins racing after her.

"Not you two," Larry shouts. "You go get his parents and meet me at the shooting gallery!"

Benny stops, but Dennis keeps running. "Can't we see first?"

"No, asshole! Go get Charley's dad!"

Amidst grumbles of "How we gonna find him?" and "Maybe he's not even here," the twins go off like obedient pets toward the picnic grounds.

\* \* \*

When Lucy gets to the top of the hill, Larry turns and runs into the woods, keeping close to the edge of the gully. The little girl dives blindly after him. Lucy loves Charley more than anybody in the world, even Mommy and Daddy.

Larry's weight slows him down, but it's still hard for Lucy to keep up because of the thick underbrush. Where the long legs of the twelve-year-old can easily step over clumps of leaves and branches, the little girl must climb over. In no time, her bare legs are lined with bloody scratches from the bottom of her shorts to the top of her socks, and her hands are cut from grasping thorny branches. But it doesn't slow her down. She's right behind Larry.

So close that when he pulls up short, she nearly runs into him. "Where is he?" Lucy looks around frantically. There's no Charley in sight.

Before she can turn back to Larry, he wraps his arm around her chest and pulls her hard against him. With both arms pinned at her sides, Lucy is trapped in his sweaty grasp.

"Hey, leggo!" Lucy tries to wiggle out of his hold, but he's got her fast. But only for the moment. He shoulda pistol-whipped her, Larry thinks. She's nearly impossible to hold, squirming and wriggling, kicking his legs and butting her head against his stomach. All the while twisting around trying to grab his arm in her teeth.

She's a little cyclone of fight and unless he's shoots her fast, she'll get away.

Since he's used his stronger right arm to hold Lucy, Larry has to reach over her with his left to get the gun out of his pocket. He squeezes her small body as hard as he can, flattening it enough to just reach the edge of his pocket … The strength of his grip crushes Lucy's chest and all her fight goes into her struggle for air.

By scratching the fabric with the tips of his fingers he's able to work the butt out far enough to slide it into his hand. Still holding Lucy tight, he raises the gun to her ear and pulls the trigger.

An amazingly loud, sharp sound cracks the air.

# CHAPTER FIFTY-THREE

The sound is loud enough to deliver its message to the milling crowds on the picnic grounds. Loud enough that they stop instantly and search the sky for fireworks. But that naiveté lasts only a moment until someone shouts, "Oh my god, that's a gun!" and a wave of confusion and fear, but not yet panic, rumbles through the crowd.

Parents reach out for children, husbands for wives, brothers for sisters, and strangers for neighbors. Everyone turns away from the sound, pushing in the opposite direction. The people holding Luke jump up, backing away without a thought for their captive, and shove their way into the crowd.

Freed from his human prison, Luke leaps to his feet and pushes forward against the tide of people. Now no one cares what he looks like; their only interest is in getting away from danger. They know instinctively that it's more important to be scared than brave.

A woman's scream, erupting from somewhere deep in the crowd, further convinces them fear is the right reaction. The forward movement grows stronger.

Luke fights his way into the advancing throng, leading with his shoulder, slipping sideways between people, moving steadily toward the wooded hillside where the gunshot came from.

*Please, God, don't let me be too late.*

* * *

The scream is Leddy Adler's. The twins have found Charley's parents.

# CHAPTER FIFTY-FOUR

The explosive power of the gunfire has ripped the weapon from Larry's hand, ramming it straight up into the air, its flight power propelling it over the side of the gully into the dry riverbed. The bullet itself soars harmlessly over the children's heads, lodging in a thick, low- lying branch.

The force of the shot tears Lucy from Larry's arms. Like the gun, she falls over the edge of the gully, hanging precariously, fingers wrapped around a ropelike tree root, legs dangling free. Deafened by the gun, she hears only silence underlined by a thin, shrill hum.

Larry is thrown back too. His body slams against the tree behind him, momentarily knocking the wind out of him. His head is also wrapped in a thick wooly silence. He can't hear himself greedily sucking in lungful after lungful of air.

\* \* \*

Lucy recovers first. Kicking out frantically at the rocks on the side of the cliff, she hunts for a ledge on which to hook her feet. Her head is high enough that she can see Larry plastered against the tree.

Finally her toes find a protrusion wide enough to give her purchase. Scrambling up frantically, Lucy keeps her eyes locked on Larry. All around her, sound has stopped.

Lucy reaches the top as Larry finds his breath. He sees Lucy; *shit*, he thinks, he didn't kill her. The best he can hope for is that he wounded her. The botched shooting is bad enough, but worse, the gun is missing. Larry thinks he saw it go in the direction of the gully. He rushes to the edge and sure enough, there it is, lying in the middle of the riverbed. All is not lost.

But he has to make a quick decision. He can't hold onto Lucy and retrieve the gun at the same time. He opts for the gun and jumps the six feet down to the bottom of the gully. As he does, Lucy scrambles to her feet and races off toward the edge of the woods.

Larry grabs the gun and is up the gully in time to see which way Lucy ran. He starts after her. She's close enough to shoot but maybe he'll miss and then what? Shoot again? That would leave only three bullets. And maybe he'd miss the third time.

Even if he does hit her, he might have to use another bullet to kill her. Shooting one kid is shit. Nobody's gonna make a big thing about that. Yeah, maybe here in Shorelane, but not on national television. No way.

Unless he can catch her and for sure use only one more bullet, he's gonna have to just forget her and go for the others.

*Fuck!*

In this instant, there's no one in the world Larry hates more than Lucy. Not even his father. Lucy Adler has fucked up everything, just like she always does. Maybe it would be worth only killing her just to kill her.

That's different from the way he feels about killing the others. Killing them is more about him. But with Lucy, it's a regular ordinary murder. He wants her gone. He wants to watch her disappear.

But he can only do that if he catches her first.

\* \* \*

Lucy feels Larry gaining on her, but she still can't hear him. Terror-fed adrenaline courses through her body; time and again she feels her breath giving way, only to have a new surge of strength fed by sheer survival instinct. Larry is big, with long legs. He will surely catch her before she gets to the edge of the woods. She has to find a place to hide.

Not a moment later, Lucy almost stumbles over the branch of a fallen tree. Ducking, she creeps through dead leaves and scrub brush until she reaches its trunk. The tree, probably hit by lightning, fell so powerfully that most of the roots ripped free from the earth. Underneath, where the dirt has been lifted, there is a small crater practically hidden by debris. Small, but big enough for a seven-year-old girl.

Lucy creeps on her belly in between the roots, digging as far down as she can with her hands. The space is too tight for her to turn around, so she just lies there, cheek pressed against the earth. She wishes she wasn't wearing a pink belt.

\* \* \*

Larry knows the little girl can't outrun him. It's just a matter of minutes before he gets her.

Except she's disappeared. Right in front of his eyes, she's gone.

She can't have reached the edge of the woods that fast. She was close by, right in front of him.

\* \* \*

Lucy can't hear Larry's footsteps, but she knows from the vibrations of the ground underneath her that he's very near. She holds her breath, waiting for him to pass. Her eye catches a slight movement in the leaves. It stops. He must have passed. Lucy exhales; with her face still tight against the ground, she fills her lungs again, drawing in moist air from the forest floor—and a tiny bug as well. Automatically she pushes air out from her nose to expel the bug. It doesn't work. She does it again, more strongly, and feels the bug shoot from her nose.

\* \* \*

Larry is still close by, stamping and kicking at the underbrush. He stops and listens. The ringing in his ears has faded, but not enough to pick up small sounds. He searches the piles of twigs and leaves. Staring hard at the ground, he thinks he sees the tiniest breeze move some of the dark bottom leaves. He's about to investigate when, in the periphery of his sight, he spots a small patch of pink.

He takes a large step in that direction, pulls out the gun, and points it straight at the strip of pink. He butts the underbrush with his foot; leaves fly up, along with a small pink belt that hooks around his sneaker. The belt, but no Lucy.

Larry looks up in time to see the little girl fleeing, charging toward the picnic field, racing for her life.

* * *

Lucy hits the end of the woods at top speed, bursts out into the clear, and keeps going, tumbling down the hillside, rolling, arms and legs curled up into a ball.

# CHAPTER FIFTY-FIVE

Luke breaks through the crowd in time to see what he guesses is Lucy's almost-unrecognizable form sliding down the hillside. He races toward her.

The little body comes to a stop. Unfolding herself, Lucy stands dizzily. She's alive!

He made it on time.

"Lucy!" Luke hurries toward her. At the same instant, Leddy and Ned come rushing out of the crowd, shouting their daughter's name. Luke stops and turns. He knows the couple racing toward Lucy must be her parents. He watches them scoop up their little girl, and then he turns to the top of the hillside to see what he already knows will be there.

Larry emerges from the woods.

Luke takes a deep, satisfied breath: he's caught him. The thrill stretches his lips into a trace of a smile, and he waits with sweet anticipation for the boy's eyes to find him.

Larry looks first at Lucy and her parents, then he sweeps the near-empty field until he alights on Luke. He stops dead, staring at the impossible.

Luke, his prisoner, alive and free. Standing upright, all six feet of him. Standing as a man.

Luke watches shock and stunned horror freeze Larry's face. Luke looks at the boy standing above him, but he doesn't see a boy. He sees only his hated tormentor. All the pain and humiliation of his days as a prisoner wash over him, and he regurgitates fury, a rage so deep, black, and visceral that it rips from his gut with the roar of a wild animal. All control and restraints fall away, and Luke rises, arms clawing the air, and charges at his enemy with enough ferocity to rip Larry apart.

Another fifty feet and he'll be upon him.

Somewhere in Luke's head, the sight of the gun registers, but the message doesn't move to conscious thought until he hears the shots.

One.

Two.

He feels the odd whack of something landing like a punch on the fleshy part of his thigh; there's no pain, just surprise. The force of the hit smacks one leg up against the other. Luke looks down in time to see blood splotching the surface of his pants, and he doesn't care.

He looks up at Larry and, savoring the kill, resumes his charge. Larry screams for help, voice high and shrill with terror, but Luke is unstoppable.

\* \* \*

"No! No!" Larry screams, the gun dangling from his hand, his head shaking back and forth as he tries to force it all away.

This is all wrong, wrong! He shot him! But it didn't stop him. He hit him, Larry knows he hit him, but the guy keeps coming. It's the guy from the sewer and he's big, really big, so much bigger standing up! Big like Larry's father. And angry like Larry's father.

Larry can already feel the blows. The guy's gonna whack him in the head first, he knows that. Always on the right side. And hard, hard enough to send that ball of air pounding against his eardrum. Then he'll punch him in the stomach and kick him and hit him in the face. And all the while he'll be screaming, "Fuckin' moron! Fuckin' moron!"

He's coming at him like an animal. He's gonna rip him apart. He's got to stop him!

Mommy!

Larry closes his hand tight around the gun and lifts it up. And as he does, all sound, even his own screams, stops. The air turns pins-and-needles numb with a thick silence.

\* \* \*

Luke's eyes never leave Larry as his legs devour the distance between them. Nothing can stop him, he thinks, savoring the power, the freedom—

And then something does.

It stops him with a power so great that it forces Luke back on his heels, skids him to a stop so precipitous that it brings him to his knees.

That something is the sight of a twelve-year-old boy standing on the top of a hillside pointing a gun at his own head.

# CHAPTER FIFTY-SIX

Daisy, frantically plowing her way forward against the panicked movement of the crowd, breaks through into the open area below the hillside. The first people she sees are the Adlers. Ned is holding Lucy while Leddy, leaning close, comforts her daughter.

Thank God she's alive.

Fifty feet to the side, Lucy sees Luke's back. He's on his knees, one hand holding his leg, his face turned up toward the top of the hillside.

Before she can follow his line of sight, Charley Adler comes running from the direction of the parking lot, racing across the grass. Though Luke is almost in his path, Charley doesn't seem to see him. Daisy watches as Charley runs into his mother's arms.

Now Daisy's eyes move to the top of the hillside. She gasps. There he stands, that miserable boy, Larry, facing straight forward in the direction of no one, pressing a gun to the side of his head.

She's stunned, motionless. From the corner of her eye, she sees the Adlers and the Duncan twins become aware of Larry. They, too, stop moving.

The enormity of the threat freezes everyone, a bizarre still life, a tranquil hillside caught in the horror of an unspeakable moment.

Though Luke hasn't moved, Daisy can see he's hurt just from the way his upper body hovers over his leg. Affecting as calm and level a carriage as she can, she starts toward him, her eyes fixed on Larry, who remains still.

As she closes the distance, Luke, unaware of her presence, rises and begins to walk slowly toward Larry.

Daisy stops and watches.

Larry moves his head slightly toward Luke. Luke stops.

What has changed this bully, this cruel, brutal boy, into a victim? The very boy that he is. Unquestionably cruel, brutal, and a bully, but a boy nonetheless. And a man must save a boy if he is any kind of man.

With that resolve, Luke begins to speak to Larry. His words start so softly that they seem to float on the air, leaving only a smooth, gentle hum of unintelligible sound. When it reaches the boy, it feels like kindness. Larry can't make out what Luke is saying, but he's mesmerized by the unfamiliar tone and watches him approach without moving.

Now Luke is just five feet from Larry. Still very far for life or death.

Their eyes lock, but the boy doesn't move. Another couple of feet, and Luke will be close enough to reach him. To take the gun from Larry's hand.

The ear-splitting screech of a microphone cuts the silence. "You do what I say, boy! You put that gun down. Right now!" Larry's eyes open wide in horror at the sound of his father's voice.

The reflex of fright tightens his hand on the gun. Luke grabs that nanosecond of distraction to cover the distance separating them. In one leaping motion, he knocks the gun from Larry's hand, and before the boy can respond, Luke wraps his arms around Larry and hugs him to his chest.

Big as he is for his age, Larry feels like a child in Luke's arms. His head only reaches the middle of Luke's chest. Somehow Luke remembered him being so much bigger. Luke can feel the heat and softness of the boy's body and the thumping of his racing heart, a pounding that reverberates into Luke's own.

What was an almost empty field moments before is now covered with police and people. Storming out of a clot of blue comes John O'Neill, his face flaming red, fists clenched, fury rasping his voice.

"Get over here, you crazy moron! You goddamn fuckin' lunatic!" Larry's body quakes, burrowing deeper against Luke. Little whimpers of terror escape his lips and sobs shake his head. In response, Luke tightens his grip and turns slightly so that the boy is still sheltered. Now he's fully facing the enraged John O'Neill, who stomps across the grass swinging his arms with an assurance that leaves no doubt as to who has taken over.

Luke watches him but doesn't let go of Larry.

"Get over here! Right now!" O'Neill shouts, slicing the air with his forefinger to mark each word.

Still, Luke holds the boy, who only clings tighter. Here, in front of him, he sees true brutality. He knows it's not the boy. What can a boy of twelve be but a poor imitation? Yet if left unattended, unchanged, the atypical cells of this vicious childhood will turn cancerous with maturity.

Never before in his life has Luke had to take the position of guardian, to be a protector of someone. Not that he is cowardly, or even remarkably selfish, but like so many young men growing up, he was simply never called upon to give more help than heavy lifting. Additionally, the special tightness of his life with only his mother—just the two of them making their own separate ways, people who asked nothing and never noticed that they gave nothing—was not conducive to the bloom of benevolence. A bloom he never knew he didn't have.

And now he is cast as father, protector, judge—and from the looks of the man bearing down on them, warrior. He feels the challenge expanding his heart, and he knows he is finally where he was always meant to be. Never has he felt so right in his own skin.

"Stop right there!" Luke doesn't shout, but his voice is loud and strong. He shoves his hand up, palm out, to accent his words. And O'Neill stops.

But only for an instant, and mostly from surprise. Men like O'Neill are used to orders taken from the outside world and dutifully eaten, only to be regurgitated in brutal strikes against his weaker family members, his wife and son.

In that brief hesitation, O'Neill has time to appraise his opponent. He finds the command belies the physical threat and Luke's bizarrely ragged appearance. He resumes his charge. Luke shoves the boy behind him, and with both feet planted squarely on the ground, forms a wall of defense with his body.

"You're not laying a hand on this kid."

"Who the fuck are you?"

Luke doesn't move.

"Get out of my way!" O'Neill is close enough to spit the words into Luke's face.

Luke doesn't move.

Now O'Neill is upon him, trying to shove him aside. Luke knocks O'Neill's hand out of the way. He has the impression there are people moving in. He waits for the next attack—two hands thud into his chest, momentarily knocking the wind out of him, but Luke stands his ground.

"That's my kid, and I'll do what I want! No son-of-a-bitch fuckin' homeless bum is gonna stop me!" O'Neill reaches around Luke and grabs Larry's arm. "C'mere, you little bastard!"

Luke breaks O'Neill's grip with a quick karate-chop knock to the arm and pushes the boy safely out of the way.

O'Neill turns on Luke with wild swings hardened by a lifetime of heavy work. He lands bruising punches every which way, all the while kicking at Luke's legs with his steel-tipped work boots, driving him backward into a tree. With Luke's body trapped against the trunk, O'Neill pounds Luke ferociously.

There are people around, police, but no one stops him.

"Watch out!" Luke shouts. For a split second O'Neill throws a look to the side, time enough for Luke to ram his fist with all his might into the soft, beer-grown girth of his assailant. The blow doubles O'Neill over, leaving his jaw perfectly positioned for the uppercut that Luke delivers with his fist.

Two life-and-death fights in a couple of weeks—and Luke has never been a fighter. He's athletic, but he's never had enough of a killer instinct to be outstanding.

But now he's fighting, not just for the boy, but for his own life—and not only the physical one.

Nobody's going to let O'Neill kill him, they'll stop it long before that, but Luke knows in his soul that if he doesn't triumph, he is as good as dead. The sewer was his nadir. Saving this boy is his salvation.

Here, now, he can show the world—show Daisy—that he is a man of substance. Not a hero. If you think you're a hero, you're automatically not. Instinctively, Luke has found a way to be better than that.

The powerful two-fisted blow to O'Neill's jaw knocks the man's head up high enough to put him in line for the perfect coup de grâce. And Luke is ready. He slams his right arm forward, aiming straight for O'Neill's head. His fist rushes through the air even with his target, but then the target slumps to his knees, arms cradling his head, and Luke's fist hits empty air. The strong response from an equal has reduced O'Neill to the natural cowardice of a bully.

When Luke looks up, the police are close by, close enough to grab him. But no one does. Behind him, Larry cowers in terror. There's no one he's not afraid of now, and that includes his savior.

"I'm charging this man with physical abuse of a child. And you people damn well better do something about it."

There's less surprise than one would think. John O'Neill's reputation is well-known in Shorelane. But it has taken a stranger, a no-account nobody, to shove it in their faces and not leave them any room to wiggle away.

"Who the hell are you?" someone blurts.

"What difference does that make?" Daisy says, pushing her way to Luke. "You all know it's true. If he doesn't make the complaint, I will."

"We will too," the Adlers say.

Worms are turning all over the place.

By now, John O'Neill is on his feet. Unless he can get Larry and get out fast, he's got big trouble. Trouble he can't handle. He pulls his son up from the ground with an unnecessarily hard jerk. His frustration and anger are too deep to hide.

"We're outta here. C'mon."

"Just a minute, John." Danny Dasto, minus his uniform but still exuding police-style calmness, steps up to O'Neill. He gently takes Larry's hand out of his father's. "This has to be settled and it can't be done here. Why don't you just go on home? I'll bring Larry over to Judge Cookson's with me. We'll work it out. And this, too," he says, bending down to pick up the gun.

Larry docilely backs toward the officer, moving more like a six-year-old than a twelve-year-old.

"You can't do that! I got a license ..." O'Neill starts, but he senses quickly that this is not the time and place to make his stand. When he looks around, he can see no discernible sympathy in the crowd.

"Go on home now. We'll work it out," Dasto repeats.

O'Neill turns reluctantly, muttering pieces of phrases in an attempt to engage the crowd, "They got no right to do this ... He's my kid ... How would you like it if somebody came and told you what to do with your kids?"

But the crowd backs off. Nothing more disgusting to people than a child abuser, even an unproven one. And guns and kids, that time is over.

Now the interest turns back to Luke.

"Just who the hell are you?" Dasto asks Luke.

Daisy answers, looking at Luke. "He's my friend. My very good friend." Turning to the police officer, she says, "Did you see the way he saved that boy's life? And believe me, that's one kid that almost didn't deserve it."

"What are you talking about?"

"Ask Larry."

But Larry shrugs, muttering, "I don't know nothin'." He has escaped the most dangerous threat; with his father gone, he reverts to his usual tricks. Besides, he sees the twins in the crowd. His twins, his lackeys and a source of guaranteed support.

"We don't know nothin', right?" He looks to them for

confirmation; of course they give it, shaking their heads and repeating, "We don't know nothin'."

To the crowd, Larry is still a sympathetic character. They take him at his word and turn with just a hint of hostility to the stranger for an explanation.

Luke looks at Larry, but it's hopeless. There's no way that this boy, conditioned by life to lie to save his skin, is going to admit what they did to Luke. Luke will have to forgo revenge and get his satisfaction from saving his tormentor's life.

And his own in the bargain.

"The hell with it," Luke says. Now that the adrenaline has receded, his leg is beginning to throb. "Let's get out of here, Daisy."

But Luke is wrong. He might get some justice after all. "Hey, mister? Mister?"

It's Lucy and she's talking to the cop. Larry freezes.

"What is it, honey?" Dasto knows Lucy well enough to listen, even though she's only seven.

"Larry tried to shoot me."

"Did not. It was an accident. The gun went off accidentally. Right?" From habit, Larry looks at the twins for confirmation. They weren't there. Still they nod their heads, yes.

But Lucy's not going to be stopped. "Yeah, well, it wasn't an accident what he did to that man." She points at Luke. "We did something bad to him, especially Larry."

"She's lying. I never did nothin' to that guy."

"He got stuck in the sewer and Larry wouldn't let him out."

"That's a lie. We tried to help him, right?" Again, the look to his collaborators, who nod. "He attacked Charley, right, Charley?"

All eyes turn to Charley. He's been there all the time, standing quietly. Now it's his turn to agree, and he can't meet Lucy's eyes.

Yes, Luke did grab his foot like he was going to hurt him. Yes, he has to say that Luke attacked him.

He knows it's not a good answer. It's not the answer Lucy would give. But Charley has to live in a world of Larrys—not just today when everyone is around but every day, when he's alone walking home from school or going on an errand or riding his bike around the neighborhood. This guy's gonna leave, and who cares anyway? He's alive; it's not like Larry killed him. If Larry killed him, Charley would tell. He knows he would.

"Tell 'em, Charley," Lucy looks at her big brother, sure he will tell the truth. But Charley doesn't answer. He keeps his eyes on the ground.

Lucy spares him and starts to tell what happened. Everyone listens. She doesn't tell it all, just the worst things—hitting Luke with rods and Larry not letting them tell. About the rain and how Luke was drowning.

Luke can't listen. He's disgusted by the picture of his weakness and the pitying looks people are giving him. His moment of glory is over. He has to get away.

And he knows where he's going.

"Daisy." He puts out his hand and she takes it. They start to walk through the crowd, which parts respectfully. He hears the children behind him.

"She's lying," he hears Larry say. "I swear to God."

And then he hears the twins back him up. "She's lying," they say. Then he and Daisy are out of earshot. In fact, they're farther than that; the two of them are out of the reach of anyone in the town of Shorelane. Forever.

At last, Luke knows where he's going. Back to Los Angeles.

Hopefully with Daisy.

# EPILOGUE

Even if Luke and Daisy had been closer, they couldn't have heard what Charley said because Charley never spoke.

He didn't lie and he didn't tell the truth, and for the rest of his life, he'll replay this scene over and over again. He'll play it where he tells the truth, and thanks to him, Larry is punished, or he plays it as it was. Whichever way he remembers that moment, the truth of it always stands as the shame of his childhood.

Lucy never mentions it. Not even when they grow up.

But the irony is that Charley didn't have to tell the truth for anyone but himself.

Everyone who was there that day already knew.

# ACKNOWLEDGMENTS

For my character inspiration I have to thank my brother, Burt Rubin, and my agent of thirty-eight years, Amy Berkower, for everything a dream agent can do, plus wisdom and loyalty. And a lasting friendship. I would also like to thank my editor, Peggy Hageman, for her sharp eye, encouragement, and excellent advice. She understood the character immediately and helped me focus on revealing him to my reader. And to Ben Patrusky, Ken Gross, Jon Marans, and Maria Guarnaschelli for their helpful suggestions. And to Hilary Bloom, Meredith Young, and Anita Anastasi for their encouragement and patience. And, of course, to my family—Molly Wenk, Mia Johansson, John Carmen, Nicole Johansson, Alice Wenk, and Thomas Wenk—for always being so supportive and encouraging.